no space for further burials

no space for further burials

by FERYAL ALI GAUHAR

Published by Akashic Books

©2007, 2010 by Feryal Ali Gauhar
Orignally published in 2007 by Women Unlimited, India

ISBN-13: 978-1-936070-60-2
Library of Congress Control Number: 2010922849

First printing

Akashic Books
PO Box 1456
New York, NY 10009
info@akashicbooks.com
www.akashicbooks.com

For Shiko

I am a wisp of straw to you, O violent wind:
How can I know where I will fall?
—Jalaluddin Rumi

We have begun to dig more graves in the shadow of the walls of this compound. The earth is dry and hard; there are many stones and jagged objects buried beneath the surface, and sometimes I can recognize the remains of a young child or a woman, a swatch of torn fabric, sometimes deep red like a pomegranate, sometimes blue like the sky above. Many times I have felt my hands stroke the severed limb of someone I may have known, the skin cold and layered with the fine dust of this desolate land. It is as if these limbs and the fragments of clothing were the people themselves, the people for whom these graves were dug, hurriedly, before more bodies began to pile up against the wall, waiting for a space for burial.

He comes to me every morning and we begin the day with an effort at conversation. Over the last few days the enamel cup he has kept aside for my tea is left cold and empty, an indication, I suppose, of depleting rations. Or perhaps he is not happy, not happy with me, with my inability to understand him, my lack of imagination, my failure to decipher his drawings on the earthen floor of my cell. He is unhappy at the seeming absence of any effort on my part to crack the code of his language.

He has many tongues, this boy. And fluid hands with which he etches the stories he tells, embellishing his accounts of war with objects found in the courtyard—shards of broken vessels, smashed bottle caps, empty vials, shattered syringes. Once, earlier on, he brought a large catalog to me, passing it through the bars of this cell as if it was a sacred text. I noticed then how nimble his fingers were, long and sinewy, almost with a life of their own. His hands and his eyes danced as he spoke, forcefully, the words tripping over his strong teeth. When he handed me the catalog I was still looking at his mouth as he said words I barely understood. His mouth worked fast, spit forming foam at the edges. I knew that he had probably not had more than the gruel of potato peels which the caretaker's wife passed around in a large bucket, her young son pulling it along on a rickety wooden cart with one wheel missing. Yet he was so alert that morning, eyes darting from mine to the book and then to the four corners of the crater-filled courtyard. He urged me in an almost comic medley of sounds and words—I recognized the broad Russian, some German, some French, and even English—he urged me to look at the book, especially at those pages he had marked with feathers and string and even a clutch of matted hair. He whispered urgently to me, like a man crazed, to consider seriously his request to get him the things he craved, the things he knew I could get for him, if only we could find a way to contact the mail-order section of Sears, Roebuck & Company from this deserted bit of hell. As soon as I began flipping through the worn pages of a 1960s collection of American clothing and kitchen gadgets and camping equipment, he turned my attention to a pair of suede hiking boots, fur-lined, an orange parka, down-filled, a pair of goggles, and a pair of yellow corduroys.

I love America, he said, and he smiled, then laughed, his mouth opening wide. Bulbul, he called himself, after the redbreast robin sang to his mother the day his father died. That was many years ago, when the war had just begun.

On most days the waiting is endless, and I find myself actually longing for chaos to hit the compound so that there is something to watch, something to make the hours fly. I have lost track of time, and other than a vague idea of how many months I have spent locked up in this cell, I sometimes think the day is about to begin when it is dusk, and then I am afraid, for none of the people here know the difference, most of them having lost even the memory of their own names. Of course Waris, the caretaker, knows everything, and his wife the cook—they are not from among the inmates here. But everyone else is crazed, even Bulbul, who looks like he is on the edge of sanity, the way he leers at me sometimes, his eyes gleaming and his lips wet with saliva. What is he thinking? What are they all thinking in this valley of the dead? What am I to think when the sun disappears behind those godforsaken mountains and night falls over the compound like a shroud? What am I to believe in when there is no one to whom I can tell my story, when there is no one who will believe it?

one

September 18, 2002

They are going to attack the compound again. I can tell by now when a raid is about to begin because of the silence which precedes it. These people here, the inmates of this asylum, may not be as crazy as they look, for they seem to sense the coming of death and destruction as acutely as animals before disaster strikes. I have watched them from my cell, the ones directly across from me in the courtyard, the ones who have found their way out of their cells since the locks were broken at the time of the first raid. I was not here then, but Bulbul told me in his combination of many languages that the looters came through a hole in the wall after the first bombing, which killed many of the men who had been let out by the staff to stroll in the compound or to get some sun. Bulbul winked at me when he described the rape of several of the younger boys, and of the old nameless crone who weaves anything she can find into her hair. Bulbul winked and grinned and wet his mouth and then held up his forefinger and thumb in a circle, passing the middle finger of his other hand rapidly through that circle, grinning the whole time, almost laughing. He stopped suddenly, when some memory slipped across his eyelids.

Anarguli too, he said. And then he was silent, as if

something had broken in him the day the marauders raped the girl he loved so deeply.

I saw him from the bars of this cell the day I was taken, having made the mistake of going on a reconnaissance mission alone, desperate to seek something which constantly slipped through the haze of my consciousness. Since my arrival in this country, I had felt restless at the camp where we waited out the days in boredom and the nights in fear. Most of us had no idea what to expect, rarely having stepped out of our homes in small towns across America. For many this was the first real adventure of their lives, hunting down the enemy, killing for sport. This was not boot camp, this was the real thing, the actual arena where all that we had trained for would unfold before us like the video games we played at the local arcade.

At the base we were told that a dissenting warlord had begun attacking the villages outside the city, many of them perched like sentinels on the edges of the surrounding mountains. I had not intended to go alone but found myself unable to endure the long days at the camp, waiting for something to happen, waiting for orders to pursue what we were here for, liberty and democracy, both of which seemed as elusive as the enemy.

Perhaps going on the mission was not really the crucial mistake. Perhaps it was the fact that I clambered out of the jeep to peer inside the large, gaping hole blasted into the boundary wall of a dilapidated building clinging precariously to the peak of the hill nearest the city. I strayed, following the rutted trail of other jeeps which had traveled this path on unknown missions. At a certain point outside the damaged wall, the ruts in the trail sank deeper into the ground and the wheels of the jeep began to slip on sandy soil. I left the jeep to see how badly wedged the tires were, and that was when I made the mistake of peeking into the courtyard of this place where I will probably spend the rest of my days, looking out at the madness around me, locked into a cell with an earthen floor and one small window with bars protecting me from the outside.

The rebel soldiers saw me as soon as I bent down outside the wall to pick up the radio transmitter which had fallen off my lap when the jeep came to a sudden halt, hitting a large rock and then sliding into a ditch. It must have been the sound of the tires slipping and the engine revving which alerted them—it seemed as if they had just looted the compound and were beginning to return to their mountain hideouts when they saw me. They dragged me to the man who appeared to be in charge, yelling orders and shouting abuse.

Even in the frenzy of the assault, I remember him carefully wrapping the charred remains of what was probably a chicken that had been hastily barbecued over an open fire. He looked at me cursorily, picked his teeth with a chicken bone, burped, and wrapped up the meat in a piece of paper he had picked up from the ground. There were many such scraps flying around the courtyard, leaves too, and feathers from the recently slaughtered chicken.

The man had come right up to me and grabbed my face with his hands, squeezing my jaws in a powerful grip. He looked me straight in the eyes and then slowly lowered his hand to my chest, stroking my uniform

as if it was silk, lingering over my name tag. He probably couldn't read, but he peered at it for a while and
then turned his head aside and spat on the ground. He
grabbed one of my arms and pushed me toward another
man who stood by, his Kalashnikov held in one hand as
if it were a reed or a stalk, weightless. The commander pointed at the rooms along three sides of the courtyard and his soldiers pushed me toward one of these
rooms, this cell, this terrible space which is like a grave,
a tomb for the living. Inside the cell they shoved me to
the ground and removed my shoes and socks, then my
uniform. They hit me when I resisted. I heard the commander yelling to Waris that I was to be kept in the cell
until they returned, that I was not to be let out under
any circumstances. That much I understood from the
gestures he made. It would take a little longer for me to
understand the words he barked in his guttural voice.

I saw the boy who calls himself Bulbul that evening,
just a glimpse of him. It must have been the outrageously
red scarf he wraps around his filthy shirt collar that
caught my eye. I stood at the bars of the small window, staring out at the courtyard, trying to make sense
of what had happened, wondering whether this was
real, whether I was imagining this insane scenario.

It started to quiet down, one or two seemingly able-
bodied men had herded the sick ones into their cells,
and a woman began to collect the odd bits of paper still
floating around in the evening breeze. I watched her
talking to a child, a thin young boy about eight, scrawny
and ill-clothed, his mouth dark where saliva had dried
in a circle around his lips. The child never answered,
but kept playing with a wooden cart that had only three

wheels. The woman did not look at him while she gathered the bits of paper and tucked them into her shawl. She just continued talking to him as if he was part of the conversation, as if his silence spoke words she could understand.

That's when I saw the edge of the red scarf float out of a clay oven fixed in a corner of the courtyard. In my confusion I thought it was a flame, for that is what one would expect to see leaping out of a tandoor meant for baking large, unleavened naan. Upon glimpsing the long, sinewy fingers which intrigue me so much now, I looked again, pressing my face against the cold bars of this cell, wondering if I had begun to hallucinate. First his head appeared, his eyes narrow slits assessing the situation, testing the air. Finally, after the woman and the child had made their way inside the compound, the rest of him emerged from inside the oven. He wore a pair of faded denim jeans and a T-shirt emblazoned with the logo of a sports shoe company. And the red scarf, which he unwrapped and then wrapped again around his neck, carefully, as if he had all the time in the world, as if nothing was wrong, as if this is the way it had always been, this state of war.

He sauntered across the courtyard toward the rooms, rolling on the balls of his feet while patting his disheveled hair into place, on a casual evening stroll. Just before disappearing into the compound he looked toward my cell, shook his head, and whistled. I kept staring at him until he vanished into the veranda running along three sides of the compound. There was nothing after that, only the wind and the dust and the rustle of dry leaves.

September 24, 2002

This is Tarasmun, this place. It is an asylum for the mentally ill, the physically handicapped, the blind, deaf, and dumb, and the unwanted. There are roughly forty inmates here—Waris the caretaker tells me there were twice as many before the raids started. Many of the men were killed in the bombing, some of the younger ones had died of illness, others of poor conditions, and still others for lack of care. Each time there was a raid, the looters would take away the medicine and whatever remained of our rations. The food they consumed in their hideouts, deep caves carved into the sides of these impossible mountains, and the medicine they sold on the black market.

Everything is available on the black market—cans of condensed milk, cigarettes, even alcohol and videos of lewd film songs with cavorting women in tight sheath like clothes. Waris says Bulbul is the one who told him this; the boy even carried a picture of one such woman in a pink shift and black Rexine boots. This picture was cut in a circle and placed in the cap of a small tin which held his many treasures. I saw it when Bulbul came to exchange things with me, offering his plastic comb and a snort of the tobacco he held in the box if I would give him my underwear. I told him I would rather die than let him strip me of my shorts, but he didn't understand, and laughed at me, telling me that I was going to die in any case, that it didn't make any difference if I had my shorts on or not. When you're dead, he shouted, you're naked in front of God. And in front of the men who will bury you.

I have never really known if Bulbul is sane or not—sometimes his kindness is overwhelming, and at other times his cruelty cuts into the flesh like a dagger.

The day after Bulbul saw me in the cell, he appeared at the small window with a dented enamel mug and peered at me through the bars. I had spent the night huddled in a corner on the damp floor, nothing but a filthy burlap sack to cover me. Bulbul handed me the mug of hot tea and then stared at my near-naked state. After a while he smiled, then extended his hand through the bars and gestured for me to offer him mine. I did so, hesitating only because he seemed to not have washed in a long time. But his hands were clean, his fingernails scrubbed and polished. I shook his hand tentatively, fearing this gesture on his part, fearing what was to come next. Who among these people would befriend me, who could I trust? Bulbul squeezed my hand for a moment, then he stroked the inside of my palm with his finger. I dropped his hand as if it had passed an electric current through the contact. When I looked up at him he was grinning, rapidly flicking his tongue in and out of his cavernous mouth. I wanted to throw the hot tea onto his face, but thirst compelled me to calm myself. He stood at the bars for a while, then saluted me sharply and left.

September 25, 2002

I am trying to keep count of the days I am here by drawing a calendar on the last page of this book which must have been a register of some sort. There is a list of medicines on several of the pages, a kind of stocktaking. The rest of the pages are empty. The book is bound with red tape running along its spine. Bulbul found it in the office, which has already been ransacked by several groups of looters. He is fascinated by the fact that I can write—he showed me his own name in the Arabic script and then asked me to write it for him in English. I did, and then I watched as he traced the lines of the letters with his finger, as if he were caressing the cheek of a young child.

September 26, 2002

This morning the soldiers came again. They were not the ones I had been captured by; I couldn't recognize a single one. It seems that anyone can gain access to this place because of the hole blasted into the wall. I watched them from my cell as they went around exploring the compound, looking for things to loot, for people to harass, women to brutalize. There is a system to these raids—Waris the caretaker does not resist them anymore, probably having learned that to do so would amount to nothing except more harshness, more cruelty. Bulbul says the last time soldiers came through the hole they locked Waris in the kitchen and took his wife into an empty cell. Bulbul had heard her cries. The child they have adopted, Qasim, does not speak, a deaf-mute probably. Bulbul says he heard him cry that night. The rest of the compound was silent, as if the tongues of all the people here had been pulled out and chopped into pieces and scattered to the wind.

Bulbul tells me the stories about what goes on in the compound during the raids. I have begun to understand his language, the combination of foreign words he uses to explain the violence and desperation of the soldiers.

We communicate in a jumble of words, even sounds, as Bulbul paints pictures of what has transpired here, what he thinks will happen, and where he would rather be: *America*, he tells me so often, and shows me the Sears catalog again and again, smiling and nodding as if his departure were imminent, guaranteed on the first flight out.

Bulbul tells me that this place was supported by the government before the country fell apart and power was hounded like a sack of grain in a famine. There was a doctor and several nurses, some ward boys, and a few janitors who tried to keep the place clean, washing out the cells daily, even airing the dirty blankets and dousing the inmates with lice-killing solution every so often. Bulbul remembers the time he was taken to the dispensary to be inspected for lice—he had protested that he was clean, but the ward boy stripped him down nevertheless and threw a bucket of cool antiseptic lotion on him. *Khushboo, good smell*, Bulbul said, taking a deep breath and flaring his nostrils. He insists that he still smells good, although I try to avoid breathing when near him. There is a sour odor in the air all the time—obviously, the janitors no longer clean the cells, the latrines have not been cleared since the first raid, and there is hardly any water left for bathing. Bulbul, in fact, is among the cleanest here, after Waris and his wife, Noor Jehan. She always looks like she has just washed, and sometimes I wonder if she is siphoning off the water in the well and keeping it for herself and her family.

The well stands in the middle of the courtyard, under the only tree which still has its limbs intact. This is where the inmates usually gather during the day, sitting under the shade of the tree, trying to remember the resonance of their own voices. The well had been covered with a wooden lid but that seems to have disappeared, and now all kinds of things float on the surface of the muddy water—once, I believe, I even saw a severed finger, or perhaps it was a twig, or my imagination playing tricks, or the distance from my window. It's hard to know what is real here—it's hard to know anything at all except the fact that the nights are longer and colder, and the days bleak and hopeless.

September 27, 2002

I have asked Bulbul to get me some more paper and some of the pens he managed to save from the bonfire that the rebels built the last time, burning everything they could find in the office of this asylum. I saw the fire rage through the middle of the courtyard, and heard the vials of medicine shatter in the heat, glassy screams of protest punctuating the deep breathing of ravenous flames.

Bulbul promises me plenty of writing material. He holds up a charred twig and scratches it along the wall, drawing a picture of a girl with large eyes and full lips. He looks at me and then smiles as he draws a heart around the girl. Then he leans forward and kisses the girl on the mouth, making a long, drawn-out sound like a man dying. I do not know how to react—I see a young man kissing a charcoal drawing of a girl etched onto a wall and I don't know how to feel. Even as I smile I am aware that there is a great sadness here, behind these walls, outside that wall with the gaping hole in it.

* * *

September 29, 2002

Bulbul tells me that Waris has asked him to help the few able-bodied men rebuild that hole in the wall. Waris believes it is the only way they can keep the looters out. I believe that after his wife was taken into that cell and possibly assaulted, Waris wants to make sure nothing of the sort will happen again. It is a good plan, to repair that hole in the wall. It will secure the compound.

It will also remove any chance I may have of getting the hell out of here. I don't know what to say to Bulbul—he looks at me as if he needs to report the day's events to me. I really don't want to know half of what he tells me—most of it seems implausible, much of it doesn't make any sense, and quite a bit is probably his own imagination. But at least it gives me something to look forward to, locked up here, waiting for this young man with the incongruous red scarf to saunter across the courtyard and disclose the day's details to me in a strange combination of tongues.

October 2, 2002

I cannot believe what has happened. It is difficult to write so soon after disaster has struck this compound. My fingers are stiff from the cold and my back aches after long hours of crouching in the corner, hiding from the moonlight that would certainly have given away my presence.

The looters came again last night. There were many of them, from what I could make out at that time of night. Tarasmun has lost its electricity connection, and oil lamps are lit only in emergencies. It was pitch dark when the sound of rushing men woke me up from a fitful sleep. My first instinct was to look through the bars but something kept me down, hidden in the corner. Perhaps it was my own fear slithering down my back and paralyzing life and limb. I could only hear what went on—I heard Waris shouting to his wife, I heard her as she rushed past the cell, the child Qasim probably running along with her, the irregular squeak of his three-wheeled cart sounding like a fingernail against a chalkboard. I heard other voices, guttural voices belonging to men I couldn't see. There was more shouting, then the clanging of metal doors, then the wailing and screeching of the inmates I had begun to know by sight. I could not identify them from their sounds of anguish, I only knew that they were terrified. There were gasps of pain and the sound of whipping and kicking. I heard Waris yelling again, asking someone to let these men go, that they were miskeen, innocent. They could not be blamed for the war.

Waris must have been gagged. I did not hear him again, except for muffled sounds and the stifled thwack of a slap. I heard men crying, some shouting incoherently, using words I had not yet understood. There are so many languages here, and the only one I have managed to understand is the one which speaks of fear.

October 3, 2002

Bulbul has not come today. I do not see Noor Jehan the cook or Qasim the mute. It is cold in this cell where the sunlight rarely creeps in. I have not eaten since yesterday.

October 4, 2002

Nobody walked in the courtyard this morning. There

are no sounds here, only the wind and the leaves and the branches rubbing against each other. Where is everyone? Am I alone now in this godforsaken bit of hell?

October 5, 2002

Thank God Bulbul brought me a cup of tea. Thank God he is well. Thank God for his red scarf and the willing grin which curves around his face like a crescent.

Waris came to me today. This is the first time this man has actually come across the courtyard to talk to me. He is not very old, nor too young, but incredibly impressive even in his tattered turban and weathered wool vest. Bulbul calls him *Graan Kaka*, Elder Uncle. It is a term of respect. This much I have learned here, that uncles and aunts do not have to be relatives. They are family, even if they have never seen you before. And they take you into their lives as if they had always known you.

Waris has provided me with a set of clothes to keep me warm and to keep me from shaming myself in the presence of his wife. His eyes are comforting and warm like cups of tea on a winter morning, and his hands are rough and capable, stringing words in the still air with majestic flourishes. He is as royal a man as I have met, this peasant who has surely seen better days, whose voice reveals that he is not my enemy, that he is hunted too, and haunted by terrible memories which replay themselves on the insides of his closed eye.

Waris speaks to me in Pashto which I do not understand. My three-month language immersion concentrated on the language of the city and of the royal court, Persian. Waris speaks a little English, learned from the doctor who used to run this place. The doctor and his staff fled during the first raid—several of the women nurses were taken by the commander of that incursion. It is said that they will never be seen again, and if they are, their families will never accept them. This is the mysterious thing here, in this land of so much conflict—a stranger is an uncle, but one's own daughter is a stranger once she has been taken away against her will. Despised and discarded, not worth the spit which burns holes in the dusty ground of tribal justice.

But that is not what Waris came to tell me this morning. He had a proposition to make, one that I did not take much time to consider. Bulbul acted as interpreter while Waris spoke eloquently, nodding his head each time Bulbul was able to convey his intention to me. I am to be let out of the cell, Waris says. I am needed to help with those who were hurt yesterday in the raid—there is a bleeding man with a gash on his head, and a young girl who does not eat or sleep. There is also a small child who has been raped. He had been left for dead, but the morning after the raid, when Noor Jehan emerged from her hiding place, she found that the boy was still breathing, lying still in his own blood on the cold floor of the cell. He is Qasim's age, possibly not yet ten. Waris does not know if he will live—he has lost a lot of blood and lay on the floor all night with nothing to cover him. The looters stripped him of his clothes, although they must have been too small to fit any one of them. Perhaps there are young boys in their ranks, children, like the one they brutalized in the dead of night.

October 6, 2002

I have spent the day in the shattered office of this asylum, rummaging through the debris for anything that
could be used to stem the blood trickling out of Sabir
Shah's head. Sabir is the one-legged man who has a face
like nothing I have seen before. It is rutted and scarred,
much like the landscape of this forsaken valley. Bulbul
informs me that Sabir was attacked while still in his village. The only man there with an education, Sabir was
accused of blasphemy by a cleric. The council of village
elders was told that Sabir had thrown the holy book onto
the ground and then trampled it with his boots. The elders called for the village council to decide his fate. Later
that day, before a judgment could even be rendered, the
accusing cleric threw a bottle of acid on Sabir's face,
blinding him in one eye, making the flesh around his jaw
fuse with his neck. Sabir was not deranged in any way;
he was as able-bodied as any of us—despite his one eye
and one leg. I do not know how he lost his other leg;
Bulbul still has to tell me that story.

In the raid last night Sabir used his crutch to hit
one of the men who rushed into his cell. The man had
dragged a young boy into a corner when Sabir swung his
crutch at him. The crutch hit the man hard, but not hard
enough, for he returned the blow with equal or more
vigor, hitting Sabir across the head with the butt of his
rifle. Then the soldier untied the string which held his
trousers up and sodomized the child, a thin, sickly boy
who hardly had any use for his hopelessly twisted limbs.
Sabir says he did not see this; he was blinded even in his
good eye by the blood spurting out of the gash on his
forehead. But he heard the man grunting and the child

gasping in pain. That was enough to suggest to us what happened last night—that and the child's devastated condition.

I did not find anything that could be used as a bandage in the office. Waris took a bedsheet and tore it into thin strips which I used to stem the flow of blood. I know we must find some antiseptic to heal the wound, but there is nothing left here. On the wall of the cell I can see the smudge of fresh blood left from the night before, and on the floor I can see where the child lay in his own excrement, stained with red.

We have taken the child into the kitchen where it is warmer. Noor Jehan is cleaning him up, she has tried to make him drink some gruel, but his lips have turned blue and his eyes have begun to roll upward. This is much worse than I had imagined, and I do not want to think what will happen without proper medical help. Sabir will survive—he has survived much worse—but this child is a paraplegic, already ill and deformed. What chance does he have to live?

What chance do any of us have if things continue this way, if nobody finds us, trapped in this nightmare?

two

We are waiting for the night to play itself out. It is colder now, and in the morning I saw the snow on the peaks surrounding us. Waris has given me his frayed shawl which I have draped over myself to keep the cold out. He lets me stay in the kitchen where it is warmer, and where Bulbul, Sabir, and Noor Jehan attend to the ailing child.

Noor Jehan rocks him back and forth and tries continuously to make him drink the tea she keeps warm on the embers of the dying fire. I can see the liquid dribbling out of his mouth and onto the curve of his bony neck. In the treacherous light of the fire I can make out the veins running under this child's fragile skin, blue rivers of hope. There are sores encrusted all over his body, ravaged by disease, wasted by neglect. He is calmer now, it seems as if the color is returning to his lips. Noor Jehan insists on wetting his mouth with the warm tea, just to give him strength, she says. She has added some of the precious sugar she has hidden in a coarse sack behind the kitchen door. Perhaps the sugar will give the child the strength to pull through the night. Perhaps Noor Jehan's crooning will keep him alive, her gentle care and the warm tears cascading down her face.

October 9, 2002

We have to dig another grave this morning, at sunrise, when the snow on the peaks seems to glow with crimson light like the cheek of a young girl. It will be a small grave, narrow but deep enough to hold the crippled body of the dead child.

It is still dark. I have stayed up with Waris and his wife while Bulbul slept propped up against the sacks of potatoes Sabir Shah managed to acquire on a recent trip to the nearest village. How he gets around with one eye and one leg is beyond me. The crutch he uses is ancient; its wood has chipped with use and age, and the rubber cap at the bottom is worn down to a thin sliver, falling open like the skin of a wounded animal. But Sabir somehow sneaks food into this compound, using resources known only to him. He is only half a man, but seems to have twice the strength of all of us here.

My fingers have grown numb trying to write in the cold, trying to reach for the warmth of the fire that went out ages ago. I have only the moonlight to guide me, and in its shadows I see the desolation of this place more clearly than I can during the day. There is no one around; the others have been quiet since the raid. It is as if the fear has been beaten out of them, as if life itself has taken a beating. I can hear Bulbul snoring gently—he is young, younger than me, a beard and mustache barely covering his elongated jaw. His stringy limbs are stretched out on the earthen floor of the kitchen like he is at home, among his own, in the comfort of his loved one's arms.

Sabir has appeared, armed with a spade and a pickaxe. I must go with him and look for a suitable place for the grave. I leave Waris and Noor Jehan to grieve for the dead boy. He will have to be bathed in fulfillment of religious obligation, and then a shroud will have to be found for him, a clean length of cloth which will envelop his emaciated body, a cocoon for the journey ahead.

Bulbul has come to me again. I am to spend the day locked up in the cell, just to please my captors in case they return and ask for me. Apparently a large sum of money rests on my head; Bulbul smacks his lips as he tells me the dollar amount demanded by the rebels for my release. A phenomenal amount, considering that no one knows who I am or where I am at this point in time. Who would have told the people at the base about my whereabouts, and who will be looking for me? Will anyone dare to venture out in this wilderness to look for someone who never really belonged to the community of men who dream of high school sweethearts and baseball games on the weekend?

This evening Waris returned to my cell and let me out again, accompanying me to the kitchen where Sabir and Bulbul waited. Noor Jehan and Qasim must have been making rounds of the compound, feeding the inmates in their cells. I could see the peels of several potatoes swept into a corner. These people have no sense of sanitation— why must they let things just rot and lie around as if there's no way to dispose of them? Everywhere there is something rotting, and even in this dry air the stench of rotting flesh hangs heavy. Perhaps the graves we have been digging are not deep enough.

I am so tired now and want nothing more than to get out. I must get out of this hellhole.

October 10, 2002

Bulbul woke me up earlier than usual today. He appeared at the window, a shadow, his red scarf tied around his head like a bandanna. When I refused to acknowledge his presence he made a clanging noise against the bars of the cell with a spade. I had no choice but to see that he carried two of these across his shoulder, one of them meant for me.

We have begun digging the ground again, piling up the earth along the wall. Tomorrow, after we have shoveled a portion of the stretch running along the damaged wall, Waris and Sabir will guide us in molding small channels from the cells so that the water which Noor Jehan uses to wash the floors can run into the ditches. Then we will throw the freshly dug soil back into the pits and mix it up to form the clay for bricks to rebuild the wall. I don't yet know whether we will bake these bricks or just let the sun dry them before we begin our task. I do know that this is good, hard work and it keeps my mind off my misery.

I am hungry now. Noor Jehan has served us gruel made from the potato peels I saw in a heap behind the kitchen door. She is saving the potatoes for the evening meal. And she promises me some sugar in my tea later on. She smiles at me, and I can see the kindness in her eyes, hooded as they are by last night's sorrow. She must have been a beautiful woman, this pillar of strength, this matriarch. But the war has ravaged her face, drawing deep lines across her forehead which is otherwise like a lush, fertile plain, full of promise.

October 11, 2002

The water which runs into the channels we have managed to dig is filthy. It stinks, and I hate to think that we
will have to churn up the soil with this effluence. I have
told Bulbul I need to take a break. Let them do it. I'm
really not interested in building a wall that will keep the
raiders out and me inside.

Sabir has devised a way to mix the clay without having
to soil our hands with the dirty water. He began by using the armrest of his crutch to guide the water into the
pits, and then proceeded to break off some of the mangled branches of the few remaining trees. With these
he mixed earth with water, and signaled to Waris and
Bulbul to fashion their own tools and join him. I sat in
the shade of the wall for a while, eyes shut, just too exhausted, until Bulbul nudged me and asked me to help.
He said they need to have the bricks molded before sunset so that they can dry out during the night.

The little mute boy, Qasim, is helping with the laborious
task of making clay bricks. He drags his three-wheeled
cart around, carrying the clay from the pit to a sunny
spot in the courtyard where Waris and Sabir shape it
into rectangles. Sabir uses the broad side of his crutch
this time to construct a temporary siding for a makeshift mold. I think I will look in the office for something
that might do the job quicker. Perhaps a wooden drawer
from the desk that was cracked open by the soldiers.
This would make a mold for larger bricks, finishing the
task sooner. Obviously these people have no idea about

speed or time or the urgency to get things done. Even
this business of repairing the damage is executed as if it
was a normal thing to do, as if this happened every day,
digging the hard earth and channeling gutter water into
pits that look like long, narrow graves in the shadow of
this cursed wall.

I found some interesting objects in the office. There is
a register with the names of the inmates and the afflic-
tions which caused them to be incarcerated here. There
is another register of provisions, none of which exist
anymore, and a small notebook belonging to the doctor who ran this place, a Canadian, if I am to go by the
maple leaf embossed on the diary. This must have been
the man who owned the Sears catalog. There are photographs of a woman and three small children in front
of a Christmas tree and a log fire. These I found tucked
into the fold of the diary. There is another picture of a
man and a woman, the same woman, holding each other
against the red and gold of autumn in the hills somewhere. There is a lake in the background. I can see the
water clearly, I can smell the wet scent of the woods, I
can hear the crackling of dry leaves.

Bulbul called me out of the office just when I was
beginning to try to piece together the life of the Canadian doctor. I could tell from the shrill tenor of his voice
that something was wrong. I rushed out and saw him
come toward me, his scarf trailing behind him like the
skin of a slaughtered animal. *Zood bia, come quickly*, he said
and grabbed my hand. He was pulling me toward the
cell where the only female inmates of this asylum were
housed. I had never been there, even when Noor Jehan

wanted me to look at the young girl who refused to eat or sleep, staring out of an opening set high in the wall of the cell. I did not know what to expect, and feared only more confusion and the incredible weight of my own helplessness.

Bulbul urged me into the cell. His hands were caked with clay, and streaks of muddy sweat cut rivers into his face. He had rolled up the ends of his jeans and I saw deep scars on his legs, burn marks, stains against his skin. There was no time to ask him about them, he was pushing me into the cell and repeating to himself the words, "*Ya Khuda, ya Khuda*," *Oh God, oh God*.

It was dark in the cell, the light from the vent hardly enough to guide me toward the corner where a woman crouched, huddled in a dark shawl. She was small, I could not tell whether she was old or young, she had her head covered with that shawl and her hands, clenched into fists, were clutched against her chest, the curled claws of dead sparrows. Bulbul walked toward her gently, as if he was approaching an injured creature. He signaled me to follow slowly, using his hands to convey the gravity of our mission.

For a while he just stood over that figure, staring at the woman, frozen like a corpse in winter. Then he bent down and placed one hand on her shoulder, softly. The woman did not move. Bulbul began to speak to her, repeating her name over and over again: *Anarguli, Anarguli*.

It was only when he sat down beside her on his haunches that he began to speak to her with other words, tender words, ones I could not understand except for the solace they carried to this unknown person hiding beneath that grimy shawl. She did not speak, she just unfurled one of her hands as if it was a flower, the bloom of the pomegranate tree for which she was named. She held out her hand to Bulbul. I watched him as he looked at her palm and carefully brushed into his hand the tiny red beads she held within. Then he held her hand and said one word to her. *Tashakur*, he said, thanking her for the gift.

Bulbul stood up after a while. There were tears in his eyes that he tried to wipe with a muddy hand. His red scarf hung limp like a broken tail.

I could hear the soft sigh of grief as it drifted out from the crevices in the walls of that cell and settled on us like a mantle.

It is evening now. The day's work has been done. My back feels as if it has been broken in two, my hands are blistered and bleeding, the rawness of the wounds burning into my palms. It is difficult for me even to hold this pen, and as I write, the blisters spill fluid onto the paper, smudging the words which in any case don't seem to have any shape in this fading light, this place of amorphous shapes and meaningless sounds.

Noor Jehan is treating us to potatoes roasted in the clay oven. There are enough for everyone in the compound, and Qasim the boy has even managed to flavor his with some cumin seeds he says he found in the basement where provisions are stored.

Waris looks at the boy as the child indicates the basement with a nudge of his head. Then he looks at Sabir, then at Noor Jehan, and then they are quiet. I don't know what any of this means. I want to eat this potato and then crawl into my cell and fall asleep under the lumpy quilt Bulbul salvaged from somewhere. Somehow he manages to find things amidst this desolation as if he was actually shopping at the Riverside Mall in Fresno. He never ceases to amaze me, and this evening when I saw him with that woman in the cell, I realized she must be the one whose picture he drew on the wall and kissed with so much passion.

October 12, 2002

Last night, when all I wanted was to sleep, to shut out the reality of what has come to pass, I found myself listening to Bulbul's story which he told me with words he made up as he spoke, words from his heart, from the deep tunnel of his longing. I believe I have been here for almost a month now; autumn is closing into winter. In these long days and nights I have begun to understand this young man who speaks with his eyes and his hands, and a tongue which weaves terrible stories.

Bulbul sat beside me on the burlap sack I use as a thin mattress covering the bare floor. He was unable to speak for quite a while, and in the blue darkness I could barely make him out as he sat, leaning against the pockmarked wall as if he was waiting for some signal to begin his tale.

I could have fallen asleep, perhaps I had. It was the sound of his sobbing which brought me back. He reached out for me and pulled my hand toward him. I wasn't sure of his intentions, but sleep had turned my limbs into pillars weighed down with lead. I let him guide my hand to his leg, and pulled away only when he began to raise the cuff of his jeans, rolling up the soggy denim where the caked mud had stained it and made it heavy.

I didn't know what he wanted, and fearing the worst I pulled my hand away. He didn't speak for a while, and when he did he spoke through a voice strained with sorrow.

My father was a farming man in a village far from here, beyond the shadow of these mountains. We had some land in that village, Sarchashma, named for the water which sprang out of the earth and nourished the fields. We grew corn and sugarcane and it was hard work trying to farm that land, but we had enough to eat and we lived with dignity.

It was after the war that things changed quickly for us. My father went into the fields one day to harvest the corn. The leaves on the trees were changing color, and birds had started leaving for warmer places. I was so young then, perhaps six or seven. I remember I had lost my front teeth that year, and my mother kissed me and told me that there was now a window in my mouth, so I could look out at life and become all that she had dreamed I would be. She said that I was growing up to be a fine young man, strong enough to help my father on the land.

I had a younger sister, Gulmina, just three or four then. Mina, we called her. It means love in my language. And Gul, it means flower—so she was the Loved Flower, or maybe she loved flowers, I don't know—I don't even know where she is now, or if she is, or if she is among the flowers for which she was named.

That day when my father did not return from the field, my mother asked me to go and get him—it was that time of day when the sky turns the color of a ripe peach and the sun begins to settle into its bed beyond the mountains. I had herded our few sheep and the cow into the shed and was waiting impatiently for the meal my mother had cooked that day. Wild spinach, yes, it was wild spinach. And bread, made from our own corn. We even had some buttermilk from the cow who had calved the previous year—we lost that calf, I remember it still, I had named it Spozhmai, full moon, because it was white and lay curved into a circle beside its mother.

Spozhmai was born in the winter. We did not have enough fuel to keep her warm, so we brought her into our own room where my mother would hold her close to us when we slept. But the winter was very cold that year, made bitter still by the fact that the trees we chopped for kindling had been destroyed in the bombing, and those that survived had been felled by the government which said the rebels hid in these trees that gave us fruit and shade in the summer and warmth in the winter.

So Spozhmai did not live out the winter, and then my father had that accident in the field. He said he never even saw it, the mine that blew off his legs. He had been picking heads of corn from their stalks to store for the winter—my mother would beat the kernels off the cob, and even my sister would help to gather them from the patch of earth outside our home. Often we would roast the stray kernels and have them as a snack. Sometimes my mother would add a bit of molasses to the corn—my father made the molasses from our own sugarcane, adding almonds and raisins to it for special occasions, like his brother's wedding which was to take place in the spring, once the snow melted.

When my father did not return I walked toward the field as if it was just another evening, as if nothing had changed. I didn't know then that my world was about to turn upside down, that it had already become something I was not familiar with, a place I did not know.

I found my father deep in the cornfield. He was lying soaked in his own blood. When I first saw him I couldn't speak, I couldn't breathe. Then the blood in my own veins started pumping and I rushed toward him, shouting Baba, Baba, what has happened? He did not speak, and for a moment I thought he wasn't breathing. Then I bent down and touched him. His skin was wet and cold, and he did not move. I thought he was dead, that my Baba had died, leaving me and my mother and Gulmina to harvest the rest of the corn, leaving us to fight the winter on our own.

Baba opened his eyes after I held his head in my hands and cried, calling him over and over again, looking up at the darkening sky in case that was where he had gone. When he blinked and looked at me I cried even louder, not knowing what was happening. I was so young, you see. Just a small boy.

Baba had stepped on a landmine which took his legs and one hand. He said he was worth nothing now, but my mother held him, shamelessly, and kissed his eyes and his forehead and then offered her prayers to God to thank him for bringing back the father of her children. She wept, but then she wiped her tears and found a sheet to wrap the stumps left behind by the blast. There was so much blood that even the thirsty earth did not absorb it. It was like the blood of the sheep the elders of the village slaughtered for the Festival of the Sacrifice. But this was my father's blood, my own father, Sangeen Khan, a man made of the hardest rock, broken into pieces like a crushed fruit.

three

It has been a good day today. We have managed to sun dry the bricks to perfection (or so Waris tells me, he knows everything) and tomorrow we will begin to rebuild the wall.

Waris took me into the kitchen again to show me something he had hidden behind the door. He was so excited he could hardly speak, and when he did, I barely understood his words, mostly just his gestures, like Qasim the mute when he wants to draw my attention to something. Waris grabbed the shirt Noor Jehan washed for me, making sure it was not infested with lice and other such creatures. He literally pulled me out of the cell this morning. I had barely managed to sleep two nights before, listening to Bulbul's story.

But this morning I was up with the few birds that still live in these trees—many of them have died or flown away or migrated to the south in search of food and warmth. The handful that still perch on the large tree in the middle of the courtyard sing the sweetest songs, melodies out of tune with the silence of this desert. I watch them sometimes through the bars of this cell and I wonder who they are singing to, and then I remember that they are birds, they are compelled to do things for no good reason at all.

Or perhaps that is reason enough, the silence of this desert.

Waris hit the jackpot, so to speak. He grinned broadly and proudly placed a battered bicycle before me. This was a bike whose handlebars were rusted, the pedals shorn of their rubber, and the mudguards hopelessly dented. But the two tires were there, flat, but nonetheless propped up the miserable machine in defiance of all odds.

I shared the man's joy and patted the broken seat of the bicycle with glee. Dust rose from it and dispersed into the still, cold air like a whisper.

There is an argument in the kitchen. Waris and Sabir are engaged in an animated discussion, and I can make out only some of it. It appears that both men are eager to get help for the asylum, and now that the bike has been found they are arguing about who gets to ride it to the nearest village. I find this quite laughable, for the nearest village has been bombed too, the homes torched, the people forced to flee. I learned this from Bulbul, he told me about Sarchashma, north of here, across the narrow pass in the mountains.

I am amazed at the optimism both men share. I am equally amazed at how they manage to carry on as if nothing has happened. Waris takes out a small tin of tobacco and offers it to Sabir, who takes a pinch and tucks it into the recesses of his mouth. The men suck on the tobacco as if it was the life force vital to their existence. Maybe that is what I am missing, a pinch of raw tobacco that is spat out in big brown globs once it is drained of its narcotic power.

Bulbul has not come to the kitchen today. I ask Waris if he has seen him. Waris nods and indicates a small trapdoor built into the floor of the kitchen. I am not quite sure what he means—has Bulbul been hiding in the basement? And what is in this basement, this place which is not spoken about openly, referred to only with quiet gestures, as if some abomination has taken place there, some terrible atrocity which cannot be told?

The argument about who gets to ride the bicycle has been resolved. Sabir will take the bike, managing to pedal it with his one leg and the crutch (muddy and cracked though it is). This I have got to see. Waris says the wall will be built tomorrow, after Sabir returns. This is the only way out, and also the only way in.

Sabir is ready to leave now. He wears his shawl wrapped around him like a shroud. And he smiles as he readies himself for the journey, crutch poised elegantly like an athlete's limb.

Waris accompanies him to the hole in the wall. He embraces this man and places Sabir's hand over his own heart, bowing his head slightly. The ritual of farewell is so graceful, honoring the last memory you will carry with you on a precarious journey.

Sabir nudges the bike through the hole. He is the lucky one, the one to get away. I have to stay to appease my captors, Waris has to stay to protect the compound, and Bulbul—he has not emerged from the basement since the morning.

In any case he doesn't want to leave, he told me. And he certainly doesn't want to go to Sarchashma where his father is buried, and where the earth holds more than the roots of the trees that shelter all living creatures from the sun and the harsh desert light.

October 14, 2002

Sabir is not back yet. I didn't think he would even get to where he was going on that rickety old contraption, a poor excuse for transport. The sky has darkened; Waris says it is winter rain clouds. He says it is good for the soil, the crops, the animals, who will drink the water collected in the craters littering the landscape. I want to tell him, what about us, what is going to be good for us, but he has already turned his attention to a boil on his leg which looks like it's about to burst.

I turn away from him. I can see the pus oozing out of that sore, red and swollen with some infection caused by the squalor we live in. I want to tell him, what about water for us, how am I supposed to bathe, how am I supposed to wash this grimy pair of clothes that now brands me as a card-carrying lunatic, the same as everybody else here. But I don't have the words, and sometimes I believe I don't even have the will to speak, to wash, to wake up to face another day.

Bulbul took my shorts the day they let me out of the cell—he'd had his eye on them from that first day. God knows what he wants to do with them, a pair of worn-out shorts. He hasn't returned them. He hasn't returned to the kitchen either, and I am almost desolate without him.

I turn back to Waris. He has lanced the boil with the sharp point of a long nail which he heated to a red tip on the embers in the grate. The pus oozes out, a river of pale mucus streaked with blood. Waris does not flinch;

he squeezes the boil until the swelling collapses like a punctured balloon, the mouth of the sore a crater. Then he wipes the sore with the edge of his turban. He turns to the grate and, taking a pinch of ash, he applies it to the sore. I am wondering at this treatment but there must be something in it. After all, these people have survived here for ages without decent medication.

Waris looks at me and smiles, satisfied that he has conquered the beast festering in his leg. Then he rises from the floor and beckons me to follow him. I do so— we move toward the trapdoor and I know that he is finally going to let me enter that space which has been prohibited to me.

I don't know about this. I really don't know much about anything anymore. I don't know what lies hidden in the basement, just as I don't know what lies hidden in the hearts of these people—my friends, my allies, my enemies.

It was dark in the basement, obviously. There were no windows, no vents. Waris carried a lantern to guide us down the stairs as we felt our way along the uneven stone walls enclosing the space. I could smell the musty odor of something sour, something spoiled. And I could hear Bulbul, whistling in total darkness.

We found him sitting on a burlap sack filled with something, grain perhaps, or flour. He didn't look up at us. Waris went over and stood before him. I remained by the stairs, wondering why anyone would want to spend time here in this dark, dank room where light and hope and all things good seem to have been kept out. It was colder here than in the kitchen or in the sunlight, the kind of cold that eats into your bones.

Bulbul sat on the sack wearing just his T-shirt and the soiled jeans. He seemed to have lost the red scarf, the only thing he had to keep him warm. He looked up at me and smiled. Even in the weak light of the lantern I could see that his eyes were glazed over, as if he was in a trance.

Waris hung the lantern on a nail in the wall and returned to the kitchen. I took his place, standing in front of Bulbul like a guardian protecting him from the ghosts that haunted him. I asked him what he had done with his scarf. He glanced at me again, then got up and asked me to follow him to a corner of the basement. He peered up at the roof. I followed his gaze. The red scarf hung limply from one of the rafters. Bulbul looked at me and then dropped his eyes to the floor. A sack of grain sat directly underneath the floating scarf.

For a while I could not make out what any of this meant, until Bulbul climbed onto the sack of grain and reached for the scarf, wrapping it around his neck. Then I understood. He was trying to tell me that he had wanted to end his life. At least that is what I thought.

Bulbul tugged at the scarf. It was firmly knotted around the beam. Then he lowered himself to the ground and stared at me, perhaps seeking approval for this whole business of hanging himself from the rafters. In my nervousness I laughed, then pulled his arm and led him to the place where he had been sitting earlier. I sat in front of him, on my haunches, and looked into his face, asking him questions for which I had no words.

Slowly, Bulbul began to roll up the cuffs of his trousers again. I did not move, having no idea what to expect. When he finished rolling them, neatly, like a track runner, he took my hand and I let him place it over the dark stainlike marks on his skin.

Sukht kard. Burning, he said. *My uncle.*

I did not understand and continued to stare at the scars. He got off the sack and kneeled down on the floor, resting his hand on my shoulder, his eyes on mine. These were burn marks, he said, from the time after his father died, the gangrene having set into the wounds, a fever burning up his life force until he was nothing but a yellow cadaver.

My uncle, the one for who my father made the fruit-filled lumps of molasses, ended up having to marry my mother after his death, as is the custom among my people. The woman he had intended to wed the following spring was taken by the rebels when they came to loot and burn the village. She was seen again in springtime, her body floating on the scum-covered water of the village well. When she was pulled out of the well, it was clear that she had been pregnant and had taken her own life.

My uncle, Lawangeen, was now my father, even though he was years younger. He did not treat my mother well—she could have been his own mother's age, I suppose, and the woman he was forced to abandon had ended up dead in the village well. So there was much anger in him, and when he took us to the city in search of a livelihood, he expected me to find work to support my mother and sister. I was still young—my front teeth had reappeared, big and firm, as you can see. But I was still a boy.

I found a job at a roadside stall selling kebabs and naan to passersby. I was to wash the dishes and prepare the seekh, the skewers on which the meat was grilled. The kebab seller would let me have a meal of the scraps leftover in people's plates in return for my work, and

I could take home some of the naan to my mother and Gulmina.

In the evening I would stand on Chicken Street—this is where the foreign people came to shop, but since the war there were not many around. The foreigners were in the city, helping us, helping women, even helping the sick and the wounded, but they did not shop much, and in any case the shops were shutting down, business was bad and times were not certain.

My uncle wanted me to sit at a corner of Chicken Street and hold my hands out to passersby. He asked my mother to put on her burqa, and to take Gulmina along too. We were to sit near a busy intersection. We were to hold our hands out and ask for money. I said that I would rather die than beg, but he beat me and told me that with the little naan I brought them, we would probably die anyway, so why not swallow one's pride and beg for some extras, some meat perhaps.

My mother was ashamed of this, but she could hide her shame in the many folds of her covering. And Gulmina was too young to know that she was no longer the daughter of an honorable farmer. She was now on the streets, earning a living like all the shameless others who had no homes and no hope for a better life.

The first time I managed to collect enough money to actually buy something, I went straight to the vendor who sold secondhand shoes on his cart, parked next to the kebab seller. He knew me—I would sometimes get him the big pieces of meat when he asked for a meal, and he was kind to me. I had seen a pair of shoes he had on his cart—they were boots, white ones, with fur on the edges and blue laces. There was a star on the side, a silver star that gleamed when the sunlight hit it just before evening fell. I asked him for this pair—I had the money, I had worked for it.

That evening when I got home, wearing the shoes like a medal, my uncle took me into a corner of the room near the cooking fire and made me take off the shoes. I thought he was going to put them away

for a special occasion, like the Festival of Sacrifice, when we would
certainly get some meat to eat.

But he did not do that. Without saying a word, he put the shoes
in the open fire, and then he held my hands down and asked me to
put my feet in the grate. I could not believe what he was doing. My
mother protested—she screamed for him to have mercy on me, that I
was just a child, her only son. What use was I if I had no feet? What
use was I if I could not leave the house to earn a living? Had one
cripple not been enough in the family? Did I not nurse your brother
when he became half a man? Did I not hold him in my arms when
his back arched with the fever that took him from us? This did not
pacify my uncle. He pushed me onto the floor and dragged me by the
feet toward the fire. Then he took the burning rubber of the shoes I
had bought and pressed them against my feet. I remember the searing
pain, and then I remember nothing.

I woke up to the smell of burning rubber and charred flesh. I
could not walk for days. My mother would clean my wounds and
change the bandage; she would apply a paste of herbs and butter.
And she would weep, her tears healing that place in me which none
of her medicinal preparations could reach.

I don't know if I can deal with this anymore, this place,
this wilderness, the obvious desperation of a people
driven to madness. How on God's good earth am I going
to get out of here?

October 15, 2002

Sabir has still not returned. It is dark now and we sit
in the kitchen, gathered around the hearth. Noor Jehan
cradles Qasim's head in her lap. It appears she is looking
for lice in his hair. I worry now, about lice and vermin
and disease. Don't know how long I will survive this.

Bulbul emerged from the basement at nightfall. His scarf was tied around his neck again. He smiled as he came and sat next to me on the floor. Then he put his hand into his pocket and pulled out a pen, an expensive-looking pen, and offered it to me. I took it—it was a Mont Blanc, gold tipped, with a man's name engraved on the side. I read that name in the light of the fire, speaking it aloud: *David Elisha.*

Waris glanced up and asked for the pen. He stared at it for a while then handed it to Bulbul, questioning him in short spurts. Then he got up abruptly and walked out the door. He was visibly upset, and perhaps he had gone to wait by the wall for Sabir's return. Bulbul just stared at the floor, not speaking. Then he peered up and told me that the pen belonged to the Canadian doctor who had run this asylum before the war. He said he had found it in the basement, lying behind the sacks of grain in the corner where he had stood earlier with his scarf wrapped around his neck. Dr. Elisha had died in the basement, a rope around his neck, the day the soldiers came and took away the nurses, killing the male staff and imprisoning him in the basement.

Bulbul returned the pen to me, saying that it would be useful for me, for my writing, for the words I try to leave on scraps of paper so that I do not end up taking my life the way he has wanted to, so many futile times.

I wanted to see the grave where Dr. Elisha was buried. Bulbul took me to the back of the compound, near the incinerator. There are several graves there, but only one with a cross stuck into the ground. The cross had been assembled from two planks of wood with some lettering still visible on them, perhaps the sides of a crate. A long, rusty nail pierces the place where the two pieces meet. The wood is cracked at that point, and the plank that nests in the earth has almost split in two.

October 16, 2002

Last night, once I was back in my cell, it began to rain. At first it was a light drizzle, then there was thunder and streaks of lightning that lit up the sky like a thousand fires. Now it is pouring, and Waris and Bulbul have gone crazy struggling to lift as many of those handmade clay bricks as they can. They are trying to get them out of the rain to keep them dry. I refuse to leave this cell. It is cold and I really couldn't care less if the pathetic lumps dissolve in the rain. It's their wall, let them worry about it.

It was wonderful waking up this morning to see the sky clear and the dust washed from the leaves of the big tree. Bulbul came to me, face gleaming, hair combed, pants clean but soggy, and wearing a woman's orange sweater instead of his soiled T-shirt. Last night, while they were lugging the bricks into the veranda running along the compound, Bulbul decided to take his clothes off and bathe in the rain, letting the grime run off his skin into the earth. Waris had done the same, except that he wrapped his turban around his groin, unlike Bulbul who had danced around naked.

I want to wash today. Bulbul says the well has filled up again, that Noor Jehan and the boy have warmed some of the water and are going to wash Anarguli and the old crone in the women's quarter. I want some of that warm water, I want a bar of soap, some shampoo, and then I want to put on a clean pair of clothes, some respectable shoes instead of the rubber flip-flops be-queathed by Bulbul, and I want to sleep for many, many days and all the nights that follow.

Bulbul has come to me again. He does not smile, and I wonder if it's because Sabir has still not returned. I have spent the day in the sun, under the tree that still drips rainwater off its leaves. Waris has helped Noor Jehan and Qasim carry pails of warm water into the women's cell. If it rains again, I'll suggest that they let all the men out and make them dance naked like Bulbul did last night, washing away the lice and the infestations of parasites that I have seen tunneling into their skins.

But Bulbul, despite his clean smell and the combed hair and the old-new sweater, has turned into his other self again. He is clearly distressed as he informs me what Noor Jehan has told Waris about the girl, Anarguli. While washing her she had seen a swelling in her belly and wondered if that might explain why the girl hasn't been eating, whether she's perhaps carrying a child, conceived of the rape she was subjected to during that first raid. I want to tell him it could be hunger that's swelling up in her belly, like a great heavy mass of yearning.

He gets up and tells me that it's Mohammad's child. Anarguli's dead husband, Mohammad. And he is happy as he says this, waving the end of his scarf in the air like a lasso. *I look for Sabir Kaka now—he come home soon.*

October 18, 2002
They came again toward nightfall. It had begun to driz-

zle; Waris and Bulbul herded the men out of their filthy cells into the courtyard, under the tree. Some of them laughed at the rain, others wept, a few even ran in different directions, rushing to get their clothes off and wash themselves. I watched them from my cell—it had threatened to rain and I had agreed to help Waris carry the clay bricks back into the veranda. But the rain came sooner than expected and the soldiers arrived with it, turning the water in the well red with blood, shooting for sport. Waris tried to get most of the men back into the cells, but a few remained under the tree watching the leaves sway in the evening breeze.

Three men were killed, their bodies dumped in the well. Their crime? They resisted the soldiers who wanted their shoes—broken, mended, scuffed pieces of leather and rubber that cost them their lives.

Waris has asked me to help him wash out a few tin drums which must have stored oil at some point. He says we must pray for rain to fill them up with water. And once we have washed the drums we will have to remove the bodies from the well and bury them.

Bulbul disappeared again. It took me awhile to guess where he could be. But he was in the basement, in the same place. In his hands he held a pair of shoes. I examined his feet—they were bare and hideously deformed, the bones crushed, the flesh turned into shapeless lumps after the burning. He did not look at me when I stood before him. He cradled the shoes like a pair of newborn lambs, tender and fragile and deeply loved.

four

This morning Waris stood outside the cell and yelled, calling me over and over again: *Firangi, Firangi*. He waved frantically in the direction of the wall. I thought I was still dreaming, or at least hallucinating, when I saw the caravan of motley creatures amble through the hole in the wall. There was a dark-haired camel, a very scrawny mule, a long-haired dog almost as high as Sabir Shah who then walked through, crutch under his arm, a broad smile stretching like a washing line across his face. He followed the mule, patting it gently on its bony back, encouraging it to step over the debris and the sodden earth that lay in its path, a major obstruction for an obstinate beast.

I flung on the shawl and rushed out barefoot in my excitement. What was all this about? Where had Sabir come across these creatures? Which godforsaken corner of this valley had yielded such a rich harvest?

Sabir stood by the well and propped his crutch against the solid trunk of our only living tree. He continued to smile, looking at Waris, his one eye glinting with delight. Waris rushed forward and embraced this one-legged, half-blind man who had brought back gifts of grain and fruit and sustenance, bundled carefully into the saddlebags thrown across the backs of the camel and mule.

I joined the two men and we laughed together, Waris

and I, in amazement, Sabir with the sheer joy of having achieved so much more than he had set out to do. Waris called out to Noor Jehan and Bulbul and proceeded to find moorings for the straying animals. I helped him pound a couple of wooden pickets in the corner of the courtyard, across from the tandoor. We tied up the camel and mule after relieving them of the generous load they had carried across so many miles.

Noor Jehan brought out a cup of sweetened tea for Sabir. He drank with obvious relish. His face was layered with dust, his eyelashes blond from the sunlight, but his pleasure was impossible to miss beneath the grime and fatigue. He turned to Bulbul and instructed him to take care of the animals—after all, they had journeyed long to come home to all of us.

This evening we have eaten well. The saddlebags tied to the backs of the animals were like bottomless wells serving up unexpected treasures. The mule had carried a bag full of apples, most of them bruised and worm-infested, but apples nonetheless, and several pomegranates which Noor Jehan took and put away. In the other pouch there were four chickens, their legs tied to each other. The camel yielded wild spinach, walnuts, watermelon seeds, ears of corn, and potatoes. And the dog, that huge mastiff with the frayed rope tied around his neck, the dog carried his own burden: a red-beaked partridge sitting in an intricately woven cage. This was tied to the rope around his neck and suspended like a bell.

Sabir feeds the bird tiny seeds of rye and barley that he fishes out of his pocket. He has named it Inzargul, the flower of a fig tree, and as he sips his tea he tells us of his journey to Sarchashma, beyond the impossible mountains.

At first, I had a difficult time keeping my balance on that bicycle, but after a while I managed to get the rhythm of using the crutch to pedal. I wedged it between the plates of the pedal and then off I went, shooting over the track toward the pass between the black mountains. It was only after I reached the part where the road begins to climb that I had to dismount from the bike, but I kept it with me, pushing it along and actually using it to rest against when I got tired or winded.

Getting through the pass was difficult not only because of the rough terrain but because of the rebels hiding in the caves along the side of the narrow opening. I know the less traveled paths, the ones I used to take when I came from the city to visit the family, so I was safe, although the journey took more time and effort.

Imagine my horror when I got to the village: there was no one around—the houses had been razed to the ground, the crops burned, everything destroyed. I threw the bicycle down and rushed into the lanes, calling out the names of friends and relatives I had lost touch with since the accident. Khaistamir! Hamesh Kaka, Gulabsher! But there was no answer, only silence and the sound of the wind and dead leaves rustling. At first I didn't know what to do, so I sat outside the door of what used to be our home, and I wept. I know the boy Bulbul told us that the village had been destroyed, but I didn't want to believe that—how could brother turn against brother, killing and looting and dishonoring our sisters, our mothers? But it was true, the boy had told us about the rebels coming and demanding food and shelter, and when the elders decided to resist, to keep whatever meager harvest they had gathered in the year of misery, this is what happened, the total destruction of the village.

But where have these people gone, I asked myself, sitting outside that familiar door. Where could my ailing father, my sisters, where could they all have gone? And what about the animals—were they taken too? Did the rebels take the animals, did they kill them, or did my father herd up the sheep and cattle and drive them away from here, far from this desolation?

That was when I head the barking. It was the most beautiful sound I had heard in so long. It was the dog, this one I have brought with me, the one I raised as a pup, and he was barking, letting me know that all was not lost, that some of the ones I had loved were still there in their homes, even if there were no roofs on the houses, no walls left standing, but a home is where you have buried your heart, and I had buried my heart in the soil of my home the day my father asked me to leave, the day my life ended and another man, half a man, was born.

Here one's view of the world changes when one has a full belly. After last night's meal I slept deeply, not dreaming, not even shifting in my bed. Perhaps this is because Bulbul helped me make a mattress out of piles of dried leaves and the feathers of slaughtered chickens. But more than that, it's the sense of well-being that has come to me since Sabir's return—I have begun to feel that there is hope yet, that we shall be found, that there are good things to look forward to, that I am being looked after by these people here, the one-legged man, the mute child, the half-crazed, scarf-wearing vagabond, and Waris, the only man with all his senses intact. And Noor Jehan, how can I forget this woman, this mother of all mothers, the one who gets up first and sleeps last, making sure that all of us, the sane and the insane alike, are fed. Noor Jehan—Bulbul tells me her name means Light of the World, and truly she is that.

* * *

Noor Jehan came to me today. She brought Qasim with her, and while she spoke to me in her language the boy looked at the pages of this diary and began to draw with the pencil I have almost worn down to a little stub. I watched him as he drew, transfixed by his ability to turn the empty pages of this book into a world peopled with creatures real and imagined. I could not understand much of what Noor Jehan was trying to tell me, but the name Anarguli caught my attention and I realized she was talking about the girl Bulbul had taken me to see several days ago. Tearing my gaze away from Qasim's fantastic drawings, I followed Noor Jehan into the women's quarters, completely incapable of imagining what I would find there.

Anarguli sat with her back to us in her usual position. She did not move when we entered the cell. Behind her was the old woman Bulbul had told me about—the one who had been assaulted. This was a very old woman, if I could judge from the deeply etched lines on her face, like cracked earth in a drought, and the empty cavern of her mouth. She wore a frayed veil on her head, but I could see the hair—silver, thick, matted, and long, stretching to her feet and beyond. I was fascinated by the braid she had plaited—there were twigs and colored threads and bits of dried grass woven into thick strands intertwined with each other. The woman sat behind Anarguli, her knees wedged into the girl's back. I could see her picking threads off Anarguli's shawl. She twirled a thread between her fingers, then licked it and proceeded to weave it into her braid. Anarguli remained completely still, as if she was made of stone, a fossil in this airless cell.

Noor Jehan sat beside Anarguli and reached for her face. The girl flinched. Noor Jehan asked me to sit close to her, facing the girl. I did so. Qasim kneeled by the door of the cell, playing with the wheels of his cart. I could hear their whirring, and I remembered that I had promised myself that I would find something with which to build the fourth wheel of this child's precious vehicle.

Noor Jehan drew my attention to the girl's face. I leaned forward and she pulled Anarguli's veil off her forehead. I was overwhelmed by the girl's beauty. She was pale, but the coloring of her dark hair and eyes and the shadow of her lashes made her radiant. I didn't know what Noor Jehan was trying to tell me. She motioned for me to come closer and examine the girl's eyes. I inched forward, uncomfortable on my haunches, and peered into the girl's face. She did not move, neither did her eyes, and I was troubled by that. She seemed to stare at some far corner and only shifted her eyes when she heard us moving around her. I asked Noor Jehan to lead the girl closer to the window so that I could observe her in the light, the little that creeps in through that small opening high up in the wall.

Noor Jehan pulled the girl forward. She did not resist. I moved toward her and pulled the lower lids of her eyes down, looking for signs of disease. I tried to remember the many things we were taught in school at the San Joaquin Valley Central. I had trained as an emergency medical technician, and in this most distressing time of my life I couldn't remember half of what I had learned. All I could see was that the girl was anemic, almost bloodless, her skin translucent and her eyes vacant. But there was something else that bothered me

about her eyes, the fact that she didn't follow our move-
ments, that her pupils didn't constrict when we turned
her face toward the light.

I wanted to leave the cell, unable to do anything to
assist the girl, or to help Noor Jehan understand her silence and her almost catatonic state. When I turned to
exit, the old crone grabbed my shin with a bony hand
and held on with all her strength, strange animal sounds
spilling out of her mouth like gravel. Noor Jehan spoke
to her gently and tried to loosen the clawlike grip of
the woman's hand around my ankle. But she held on
with unexpected vigor, and I stood immobile, listening
to her guttural noises, watching the spit dribble down
her chin. Noor Jehan called to Qasim who stood a safe
distance by the door. She asked him to help lead the
woman back into the corner of the cell. I stood rooted to
the same spot, watching the mute boy assist his mother
in this task. Qasim seems to have a way with the people
here, locked up in his silence much like they are in these
cells. The old woman listened to him as he made simi-
lar incomprehensible sounds, touching her shoulders and
stroking her hands which were still clasped around my
ankle. Gradually she released the pressure on my leg and
I felt the blood rush into my foot, nearly frozen from the
cold and the iron grip of this crazed woman.

As I turned toward the door of the cell the old crone
uttered something, a few words that Noor Jehan seemed
to understand. I swiveled around to face her as if I too
had understood her command. She stared at me for a
moment. Then she lunged toward Anarguli and clutched
the girl's veil, pulling it off her head. Anarguli remained
motionless. Noor Jehan rushed over, a small gasp leav-

ing the girl's mouth, a sudden, sharp intake of breath. She embraced Anarguli and hurriedly put the veil back on her head. I heard the old woman babble on about something, pointing to her own head and then to Anarguli. I didn't turn back toward Anarguli, for I felt the shame that must have stabbed the girl deeply enough for her to let out a cry, a piercing sound which momentarily filled that dark room, a lament for a lost love.

When Noor Jehan and Qasim joined me in the courtyard we did not talk or even look at each other. What could I say about having just seen a beautiful young girl with tufts of matted hair growing between bare patches of skin black with dried, bloody scabs?

I don't know if Bulbul knows about this, whether he has seen the ravaged scalp of his beloved. Even if he has, he probably loves her just as much, for these people here seem not to care about anything except the deep suffering they share, the unspoken agony of their lives.

I have not slept well the last few days, and it isn't the fact of my incarceration alone that keeps me awake through these oppressive, cold nights. I cannot fathom how long I will remain here, but that isn't the only thing which troubles me. It's not just a question of not having a decent meal or proper bed to sleep in, or even the knowledge that nothing is certain here except death. What nags me most are the things we were taught before we arrived in this land, the tenets of war, the rules of engagement. I keep going over them in my head, the virtues of our coming here, the need to liberate these people, the absolute necessity of enduring freedom.

Enduring Freedom.

Enduring.

Freedom.

Two words that don't mean anything to me anymore.

This morning Noor Jehan stood at the bars of this cell again. I wanted to pretend that I didn't see her, but I knew she came to ask me for help, and I know it's for the girl Anarguli that she appears before me with such regularity. I haven't had the heart to ask Bulbul about the wound on the girl's head—I also don't have the words or the will to do so. Somehow I want Bulbul to love this girl as much as he does without damaging the illusion he bears about her, or about himself. He told me once that as soon as the war was over he would take Anarguli away from here and marry her, find a job in the city where she would become a seamstress, and they would be the parents of many fine sons. He told me that he would go to the city and look for his sister Gulmina, bring her to their home, and find her a good, noble husband.

I wanted to tell him that none of this would ever happen, that his sister was probably dead or living in some cave as the mistress of one of the commanders, and that the girl he loved so much was likely to go blind because of the head injury she had suffered at some point in her wretched life. I wanted to tell him that Anarguli would probably never be able to stitch fine clothes for their many sons, that soon she may not even be able to see him when he sits beside her on the cold floor of her cell, holding her hand and speaking tenderly of his love and her beauty.

But I didn't tell him any of this, and I didn't know

what to tell Noor Jehan who stood before me silently, her smooth brow marked with deep furrows of distress.

In training at San Joaquin Valley Central, we never learned about the kinds of injury and disease that can be expected among people who have lived with so little. At boot camp we never learned that in war the victims are always the poorest, the ones who have no choice, no power, no weapons with which to defend themselves. And at the base where our commanders briefed us on protecting the territories we had liberated, we were not told who the enemy was, and who were the victors.

I had been stationed with the Combined Joint Task Force at B— air base since coming to this strange country. We treated the wounded and the sick, those injured in the course of duty and those hurt for just being at the wrong place at the wrong time. There was the ten-year-old girl Zarmina, I remember, who came to us with one of her legs blown off and the other so terribly damaged that it would have to be amputated. She was bleeding so heavily that the doctors at the army hospital thought she wouldn't make it. One of the frontline ambulance drivers had brought her in. The stretcher she was carried on was drenched in blood, and she was so pale we thought she was most certainly dead. The commander and the surgeon at the combat support hospital also didn't think she had half a chance at survival, and when tests were run, the laboratory technicians found she had dangerously low levels of red blood cells. Instead of 40 or 50 percent, this little girl only had 10. The medical laboratory team knew they had to get the life-saving red blood cells back into her system, but when the surgeons pumped two units of predonated blood into Zarmina's thin arm, things started going wrong. Massive transfusions dilute the serums in the blood that help it to clot, and the only thing to do in order to save her life was to give her whole blood, along with units of fresh-frozen plasma.

The problem was that the lab didn't store whole blood, so we hurriedly set up a makeshift donor center and called for volunteers. Within half an hour we had four units of blood from four donors. It took longer to thaw the frozen plasma, but the surgeons had stabilized the girl and there was hope now that she might survive.

Zarmina's condition was so critical that two units of whole blood were transfused into her body that day without being tested for compatibility. We were lucky that the blood type matched, just as she was lucky to have been found by the medical evaluation team on board a helicopter, flying over her home province on a reconnaissance mission. I don't know where she is now, that little girl whose father held her and wept like a child, unashamed and unwilling to let her go. She thanked us when she left, straddled on her father's back, holding the toys given to her by the nurses and medical technicians. She said she wished she could come back for the ice cream and other treats she had been given. But in my heart I prayed that she need never see us again, not in that hospital, not in war, not even in peace.

I do not know what's causing Anarguli to lose her sight. When Noor Jehan insisted that I examine her, I asked her to lift off the girl's veil, revealing the wound which had festered and lay open like a gully. It could be the trauma of the injury or it could be disease, or even the sheer poverty of these people. Blindness can be caused by so many things, but the worst is the blindness of those who can see and who do nothing with that gift of sight.

I instructed Noor Jehan to clean the wound—I will not touch this girl unless absolutely necessary. She brought a small enamel bowl filled with warm water, and I asked her to retrieve a clean piece of cloth and some ashes from the cooking fire. She gathered them, along with a small packet of yellow turmeric powder that we mixed with the ashes and the water to form a paste. Noor Jehan applied this balm to the wound, then she blew on it, as if her breath would cleanse it of the bacteria thriving in its rawness. As I turned to leave, she pulled the girl's veil over her head.

The old crone was silent today. I cast a cursory glance at her—she was fast asleep in her corner, the grotto of her mouth wide open and her absurdly long braid wrapped around her legs like a thick iron chain. She snored gently, dreaming of another time, another place.

Waris told us last night that he expects a raid soon. It has been several days since Sabir's return, and surely someone must have seen his cavalcade of animals passing through the mountains. There were many caves along the way and sometimes when people are forced to flee their villages, they live in these caves, raising their children and burying their dead as if there has been no disruption at all in their lives. The rebels, too, hide there, and surely someone would have seen Sabir herding the camel and the mule and the dog through the narrow passage leading to Tarasmun.

* * *

Bulbul has found a way to utilize Sabir's motley crew
of animals in the construction of the wall. Waris insists
that it must be repaired before nightfall. I am not sure if
I want to be a part of this exercise; this is the only way
out, and God knows how desperately I want to get out.
I have no idea where I'll go, or how I'll get to where
I want to. All I know is that I cannot languish in this
prison anymore.

Bulbul has managed to work out a relationship with
the camel and the mule. He has built a contraption with
planks of wood from the shattered desk in the office and
wedged it on the camel's hump. Waris and I are supposed to load the bricks onto this carrier, and Sabir will
lead the mule to the wall where we have dug a separate
pit for the clay slip we will use to bind the bricks to each
other. The mule, which Bulbul has named Gulab Jan,
the Rose of Life, has probably been starving and is nothing but a heap of bones and mangy, patchy hide. But he
is useful for simple things like hauling a pail of slip to
where Waris lines up the bricks in the damaged part of
the wall. This is a patient beast, or maybe it is too tired,
or perhaps it really couldn't care either way. He stands
obediently beside Waris until the slip has been used to
plaster the bricks, and another pail needs to be filled
and carried over to the master bricklayer.

The camel, on the other hand, is a willful creature
and does not understand the commands which Sabir
speaks with great authority. Either that or it is deaf or
just plain malicious. Every time we want him to kneel
down so that we can begin loading the bricks on the
wooden platform, he decides to go for a stroll around

the courtyard and heads straight for the only living tree which still bears leaves even in this season. Sabir limps after him while Bulbul tries all kinds of whistling and calling, but this animal doesn't heed them. After much cajoling and coaxing (Sabir pulls out a lump of brown sugar from his pocket from time to time and lets the camel take a lick), the camel is brought under control and the wall is ready to receive the gift of our endeavors, the clay bricks fashioned from the soil of this desecrated land, mixed with water that has washed the excrement of forsaken men.

We have almost finished placing the bricks along the gap in the broken wall. It is evening now, we are tired, and it is not easy to continue this work in the dark. It has become much colder these past few days; frigid wind finds its way through the mountain passes, traveling over snow-capped peaks and snowed-in valleys until it finds this desolate courtyard to play its solitary game of hide-and-seek.

Waris thinks that we have done enough for today. I think we have done more than we should have—the wall is almost solid now and too high for me to climb, too slippery and wet and fragile to take the weight of a grown man. But it may keep out the rebels—at least it will not let anyone prowling around at night creep into this compound and vandalize what is left of it.

I do not know what will happen now—I do not know how I will ever leave this place. I know Waris will never let me go—he keeps an eye on me as if I am the key to the calamities this place has been struck by. I know he is just trying to ensure that the rebels will find me in my cell when they do come. I know he is trying to protect himself and his family. I know that I am his friend only during the certitude of daytime when the sun lights up the courtyard, or when I can do something for the injured, tie a tourniquet, flush a wound. I come in handy for the digging of graves, and I am looking after that girl in the women's cell. But beyond that I am Firangi, a foreigner, unwelcome and unwanted, except for the ridiculous price placed on my head.

I don't even know if I can call Bulbul a friend. It has been many days since he sat in my cell and talked to me in his strange, concocted language, days since I have seen him with that defeated look in his eyes. Perhaps I should sit him down and tell him that I have to find a way out of here. Perhaps he will assist me if I tell him that I can help him and the girl get away too.

A few days ago I asked Bulbul to explain to Noor Jehan that the girl Anarguli needed fresh air and also the healing power of the sun, that she should be brought out of the damp cell and made to sit in the courtyard. Noor Jehan agreed, but the old crone made such a fuss about being left alone in the cell that she was also brought out to sit beneath the tree.

Bulbul tells me the old woman's name is Hayat, Life, and that she has been here for most of it—her life, that is. He doesn't really know her story but believes she was brought here by someone who saw her begging in the middle of the bus depot in the city. She did not speak coherently, so she was brought here to this place where there are others like her, mute, deaf, blind, crazed, homeless, and generally unwanted.

I am not sure whether what Bulbul says half the time is imagined or if these things actually happen in this place. He says that the man who brought Hayat to Tarasmun knew Waris and told him her story, begging him to keep her here because she would most certainly have died in the desert, where she had told him she would be taken and abandoned. She was a foreign woman, a Firangan, and it was dishonorable to treat one who has come from afar with no compassion. She had been brought to a village in the north by a cameleer, Haji Allum, who had taken his animals on a ship to a land far away—the camels were to carry provisions and metal tracks for the new railway being laid in that country. There were others in that country who had also come from afar, working hard in that hard land, dreaming of the homes they had left behind. When they needed money at the end of the month, before their English master paid their wages and after the stupor of their drunken state had worn off, they would borrow money from Haji Allum. When one of these men could not pay Haji his interest or the amount borrowed, Haji just took his young daughter and brought her back to the homeland on the ship.

Haji Allum died shortly after reaching his village—they say he became ill with a great fever while at sea and did not live for long after the end of the journey. His wife, the Firangan, was given a new name by his family, Hayat, and when Haji died, his father thought it best to marry her off to his nephew. But Hayat resisted, and on the night of the marriage ceremony she tried to cut off her wrist with her husband's chaakoo, the knife he used to whittle reeds for the birdcages he had been making on the journey home. She had bled so much that

the family thought she was dead. When the women began to wash her body to prepare her for the burial, they
saw that she had thick, dark hair all over her body, even
between her breasts, like a man. And there were compli-
cated tattoos that covered her arms, something no one
in that village had ever seen before. There was even a
tattoo on her mouth which made it seem as if she had a
mustache—thick, dark, twirling whiskers.

Just as the women were completing the ritual and
wrapped Hayat's body in its kaffen, the burial shroud,
she moaned and moved her head, trying to breathe
through the white covering. The woman who would
usually take care of the ritual cleansing of the dead body
ran out of the room, screaming that this was not a human corpse, it was the body of a nekhnaa, a witch. She
refused to wrap the rest of the kaffen around Hayat and
no one else had the courage to finish the task. So Hayat
sat up, half naked and half covered with the white cloth,
and began to talk in a strange language no one could
understand. Her father-in-law proclaimed her to be a
practitioner of black magic; he accused her of being the
cause of his only son's death, of being responsible for
the drought that had destroyed their crops, and also for
the deaths of so many children from unknown diseases
which had spread throughout the village ever since she
had arrived. He pleaded with the council of village elders to banish this evil creature so that no more harm
would come to his family and to the village. The council
decided that she be taken far away from the village and
left in an isolated spot, blindfolded, so that she could
not find her way back. One of the men entrusted with
leaving her in the desert took pity on her and put her on

a bus headed for the city. She has been here since then.

Her name was not really Hayat, Bulbul said, it was some other name, some foreign name which sounded like *Hayato*. He knew that because she had spat it out at him one day when he teased her about her long hair and the various things she braided into it. He had dared to touch her braid, pulling it to see if it was real, and she had lunged at him, threatening to claw his face, and repeated her name over and over again: *Hideko, Hideko, Hideko.*

That's what her name was, Bulbul said, her real name, the name her mother must have called her by when she was still in her own home, safe and warm and comfortable.

Sabir has called a meeting in the kitchen. I don't know what this man wants to tell us, but I will certainly try to listen and understand his words since he is the only one who has managed to get anything done here. Or at least he is the only one who has stepped outside the walls of this compound and seen what lies out there, in that valley of wind and sand and bones.

I cannot sleep, and I try to write this standing up against the bars of my cell so that the moon can light up the page. I don't know why I have this compulsion to continue writing—it's not as if someone will find this garbage scrawled on scraps of paper and make sense of it. All I know is that I need to say these things which fill my head and which find no listeners among these people here. I cannot even address this to anyone I know, to anyone I love, my family, my friends. To do so would be to imagine that they will receive this ridiculous record of events taking place in an asylum for the mentally ill. And much as I feel that I have perhaps earned the dubious distinction of being rightfully among the insane in this place, I know I haven't completely lost my mind, and I cannot suppose that anyone will ever come to know what has gone on here. None of this will figure in any historical narrative of our country's military achievements in the twenty-first century, no one will know about the lunacy of this war, and no one will care to learn about the courage of those who fought for their lives with nothing in their hands and only some kind of misconstrued hope in their hearts.

The bombing began late at night. I did not hear the aircraft passing overhead. It was the massive explosions that jolted all of us out of sleep. One corner of the compound was hit—I heard the huge blast and then the sound of screaming and barking and braying. Then a deep silence. The second time the compound was hit, I could actually hear the whistling sound of the explosive hurtling through the air. The second bomb did not detonate. We saw it in the morning, lying half-buried in the debris of the shattered building which housed the patients. No one wanted to go near it, not even the sick ones. Waris and Bulbul and Sabir occupied themselves with digging bodies out from beneath the collapsed walls and roof. There were many bodies. Those who survived sat on the debris and under the tree (one of its branches caught fire last night—I don't know how it survived). It is as if they have no idea what happened here. Perhaps that is better. Perhaps it is better not to recognize the bodies of men one sat with the night before, sharing a meal served in dented tin plates.

We have pulled out several bodies of children too, hopelessly mangled under the weight of the concrete roof which collapsed on them while they slept, wrapped up in the filthy gray blankets that Noor Jehan tries to air on sun-filled days. Some of the children had soiled themselves in the night, leaving dark stains of urine alongside the blotches of blood where they were crushed.

By midday the heaps of bodies and blankets smelled of burned flesh and excrement. We will have to dig more graves now, before sunset, and find a place to house the survivors so that they do not freeze to death in the cold night air.

There were twenty-three bodies—eleven children and the rest adult men. My back feels like I have a steel rod inserted in my spine, and my hands are blistered so badly I cannot clench my fist or even curl my fingers around this pencil without wincing.

We did not dig separate graves for the dead. There was no time—burials have to take place here before sunset, and in winter the sun sets early. Waris suggested that we bury them along the wall where we had dug the ditches for the clay. The ground is still saturated with moisture and is easier to dig. There is no need for separate graves since many of these bodies were not even whole when we managed to pull them out from under the rubble.

Whose names will we mark on this grave, this pit which contains the remains of children and men who had no use for war?

* * *

I cannot believe what I have seen buried beneath the debris we cleared today. I cannot believe it, or do not want to face what lies at my feet like a malevolent beast waiting to be woken up.

This morning, when Waris and Sabir and Bulbul were scouring the rubble for signs of life, calling the names of men they did not see among the survivors, and who they did not recognize among the dead, I stood beside the unexploded bomb and read the markings stamped along its iron shell. It is a USAF JDAM, a smart bomb intended to destroy an entire village, 2,000 pounds of deadly explosive packed into a cylinder bearing a message scrawled in marker on its side: *Hijack this, fags.*

There is a name beside the message. I do not want to read it. I do not want to know who it is—I might have sat with him one evening and he might have showed me a picture of his girlfriend and told me that she would be waiting for him when he got back from this godforsaken hellhole.

At the top of the cylinder is the flag of my country, marked clearly and with so much pride.

five

I remember a day when my mother was speaking to my sister on the phone at the beginning of the war. Suddenly her face turned pale, her hands trembled, and she put the phone down and turned toward me, distraught and unable to speak. My sister was eight months pregnant and while she chatted my mother, a car had arrived at her front door. She whispered something about a "government" car, and my mother understood. She waited for my sister to return to the phone. All she could hear at the other end was my sister's hysterical screaming, repeating the words *No, no, no, it can't be, it can't be*, over and over again. My sister's husband, a KC-130 tanker pilot, had been shot down.

When they come to inform the family, it's as if there is no need for words. It is quite enough, I am sure, for the wife of a military officer to see a chaplain and a man in uniform at her front door, waiting for that door to open and for that woman's life to change drastically. I am sure the words sound quite hollow in any case: *We regret to inform you that your husband, First Sergeant so and so, was killed in the line of duty in such and such . . .*

I did not intend to join this war until the day we buried Carlos Negrete. I had other plans. I had a job in the public library and I had spent many silent hours reading and imagining the places drawn out by a writer's steady hand. I wanted to go to college, working nights, working hard. I wanted to be a writer, but had never imagined that I would begin by writing on bits of paper salvaged from the wreckage of a place a million miles from anything I have ever known.

Life showed me something other than my naïve belief that the world exists according to plans drawn on the highly polished surface of a military officer's desk at headquarters. I am nothing now, will never be what I dreamed I could be. I am the silence that fills all the empty spaces of my heart.

We have finally cleared most of the debris. Our hands bleed and our limbs feel weighed down with lead. Noor Jehan tries to keep the fatigue away with her sweetened tea, and Qasim helps by removing bits of the broken concrete on his cart. I still haven't fixed its fourth wheel. I don't know if I want to fix anything, now that everything is broken.

I didn't want to eat dinner today. It's not that I can't face another plate of the same unpalatable gruel we are served every day. By the time we had cleared the south portion of the wrecked building, I couldn't even find the energy to keep my eyes open or swallow my own spit. I crawled back into my cell at sunset when we stopped working, too tired to ask Noor Jehan for some warm water with which to wash. I collapsed on my mattress and slept fitfully until Bulbul woke me up when it was already dark and the sky was lit with stars and half a moon.

I wanted to tell him that I wasn't hungry, that he

should leave me alone, that I was sick and tired of this place, and that all I wanted was to get out, or failing that, just to stay in my corner and die.

But Bulbul was not asking me to join him in the kitchen. He was begging me to help him—after working on that pile of debris for the whole day, he had sat near the fallen trunk of a tree and rested for a while when he heard a sound, a soft cry like a whimper. He thought he was imagining things—he had not eaten since the morning and his stomach was restless with hunger. But then the noise came again, a low groaning sound. This time Bulbul stood up and turned around, facing the bombed-out side of the compound. He stopped. It seemed to be coming from beneath the rubble. He couldn't believe it at first, but then the moaning became a little louder and he heard the words, *Ya Allah*, *Oh God, Oh God*, over and over, fainter each time. Bulbul was certain now that he was not hearing things and he rushed to Waris and Sabir, telling them that there was somebody beneath the rubble, that someone was still alive three days after the bombing. Waris and Sabir went back with him to that spot with the fallen tree branch and waited to hear the sounds of this survivor. Night had already fallen; the men were tired, and there was no sound except for the wind. They stood for a while as Bulbul walked over that patch of debris and called out to the person he knew was still buried beneath the collapsed building. But there were no more cries, and Waris and Sabir left after explaining to Bulbul that he must have imagined this, that there was no one there, no one could have survived three days without food or water.

Bulbul insisted that he was right. How can we be so

sure there is no one there? he asked me. How can we just let this person die without even trying to dig him out?

I went with Bulbul to the shattered building and helped him remove chunks of concrete from around the big branch. We didn't hear anything, no sounds, no human voice, but Bulbul insisted that we continue with the work. I didn't want to refuse him—his insistence was like a claw pulling my flesh, and if I turned away I would tear off my own skin.

We continued searching the darkness in silence. It was when we were ready to leave that the words *Ya Ali, Mushkilkusha, Ali, Ease my burden* floated up from the rubble. Bulbul rushed back to the branch and tried lifting it. It was impossible to move that massive piece of wood, wedged as it was between the collapsed walls of the building. We had to look for some other way to dig out the trapped man. That is when the dog, Sabir's great mastiff, came forward and joined us. He found us on top of the mound of debris and began sniffing the ground near the fallen branch. We let him guide us toward a shallow burrow through which Bulbul could crawl, reaching the man pinned underneath. I rushed to get Waris and Sabir and called to Noor Jehan in case she could also help lift the branch to free the trapped man. But there were not enough of us, and finally Waris decided he would try the impossible. He would bring some of the men he had herded into the basement to try to get their assistance. I thought this was a long shot—these were men who had no idea of even their names, or the faintest notion of the place they were stuck in, that deep, dingy basement in which the odor of death clung to the stone walls. But we didn't have a choice—a shot in the dark was better than no shot at all.

I have yet to come to terms with how things work around here. If there is an equation that rules the lives of these people it would be: nothing + nothing = something. That is the only way I can describe what I saw last night.

Waris managed to convince seven men to follow him out of the basement and try to lift the huge branch. These were men whose clothes had not been washed for months, they had not bathed for as long (I'm not sure if these seven did the naked dance that night in the rain). In short, they stank, they were diseased, most of them had lice, and all of them were insane. They had no idea what lay beneath the tree—they just repeated what Waris asked them to do: *Lift the branch, lift the branch.* I watched as they worked in unison with Waris as their leader, looking toward him for guidance. They did not talk, unless the sounds they made could be considered language. One of them kept staring at me as if I was someone familiar, or perhaps he was just curious about this man who did not seem to belong. Or perhaps I delude myself—maybe I do belong here now. In any case, I am a part of all this madness until I find a way out.

At that point, in the middle of the night, Bulbul managed to crawl through the rubble and pass a long rubber hose into a small opening. He told the trapped man to breathe through the end of the hose; Bulbul blew into the other end, helping to keep the man alive while we found a way to dig him out. Bulbul talked to the man, coaxing him to hang on to the thread of life which stretched between them. He now appeared like a grown man, not the child I sometimes saw in my cell when he told me stories about his life. I watched him and knew that he would succeed in his mission—he could not fail, the faith he had would sustain the man and it would see all of us through this night.

It is morning now, a clear day, no clouds in sight, just the haze of dust and smoke which have dulled the air since the bombing. We managed to pull the man out toward sunrise. He is old, very old, with no teeth and hard of hearing. He emerged from the bottom of that pile of destruction lisping and asking for a cup of tea. Noor Jehan had a cup ready—she had stood alongside us the entire time, waiting for the survivor to ask for sustenance. It seems that this is a regular occurrence in this land of conflict, burying the young and digging up the old.

His name is Noor el Din. Bulbul tells me it means Light of Faith. He calls him Noor Kaka out of respect for his age. And he takes care of this old man like he was truly his long-lost uncle, raised from the dead.

When we found him he was still wearing his glasses, patched and mended, but perched on his great beak of a nose, curved like a dagger, standing erect on his wizened face like a wall. One of the lenses was cracked, but Noor insisted on wearing them. Otherwise he was as blind as a mole and he wanted to see each of the faces of those who had dug him out, giving him another life.

Noor Jehan rushed back to the cooking fire to warm his tea while Waris and Bulbul carried the old man to the kitchen. Sabir guided the seven men back into the basement. I followed this new member of our flock inside—I needed a cup of tea, and I wanted to hear his story.

Waris kept apologizing to Noor for not having found him earlier. He said we had called out everyone's names but there had been no answer, and he had thought we'd lost Noor to the bombing.

Sabir looked up at me when Waris mentioned the bombing. I didn't look back but I felt his gaze on me for a long time, warming a patch of skin on my forehead as if a hole was being bored through it. Sabir had read the markings on the bomb—the others cannot read English but all of them recognized the flag, even young Qasim, who has a T-shirt with the same flag and the slogan *We Love Our Troops* written across it in bright blue letters. They didn't speak to me about the bomb that day, but Bulbul soon asked me about the handwritten words in marker. I read them out to Bulbul though I did not attempt a translation. I didn't want to explain what all of this was about since none of it made any sense. But Bulbul had understood despite my silence, and he said that perhaps the bomb was meant for me, perhaps the men in the aircraft thought I had joined the enemy.

I laughed at him then. No one knew I was here, locked up among these lunatics. And the bombers in those jets would have been so high in the air they would not have seen any living thing, only their radar screens, and they would have released the bombs according to the computations of the latest technology. They had no idea who they were bombing, even if the message they had sent was meant for the one they thought they had in their grasp.

But now I feel that part of what Bulbul said just might be correct—that I had joined the enemy, that I was now on the other side of this war. The only difficulty I have with this is that I really don't know who the enemy is anymore. I don't know who that bomb was targeting. All I know is that it cost many lives, and none of them was the enemy.

Noor Kaka began his story late at night. He had rested; Noor Jehan insisted that one of the four chickens Sabir brought be slaughtered to make a decent meal for the old man. There was some discussion about this—Bulbul said he was trying to get the hen to lay eggs which we could eat, or which would hatch to give us several more chickens, eventually. Noor Jehan argued that the old man needed strength, that he had suffered an ordeal far worse than any we could imagine, stuck under that tree, buried beneath tons of rubble, not breathing, not eating or drinking.

She won the argument, and came up with a broth flavored with cloves and pepper and another spice which looked like a five-petaled flower kept in some mysterious sack in the basement. We all had a taste, at least those of us privileged enough to eat in the kitchen. The men in the basement were given the usual gruel, except for the seven who had helped to raise Noor from the debris. They were brought up to the kitchen and given naan soaked in that broth. Bulbul saved the chicken bones for the dog that had found Noor. We all wished there was more of this soup, and Qasim was the one who did what all of us wanted to: he scraped the bottom of the cooking pot with a bit of naan and then licked his fingers, sucking on them for good measure.

Noor Kaka began his story after the men had laid out a tattered blanket on the kitchen floor and prostrated themselves in the direction of Mecca. I watched in silence as they offered their evening prayers, turning their heads from side to side in unison, as if they were one body with one belief—that all that comes to pass comes from Allah. Even Bulbul joined the men—he would normally skip the prayers offered by Waris and Sabir five times a day. But this evening Bulbul bowed his head before his Maker and thanked Him for bringing this old man, this newfound uncle, back to them.

Noor sipped his tea with immense delight. His measured slurping resonated in the kitchen and calmed our weary bodies, letting us rest our minds, at peace now with the solace of knowing that we had won a small battle in this great war. When Noor Kaka spoke his voice rasped softly, as if the dust of his underground vault had eroded the lining of his throat.

You do not remember me, Waris my son, I have been here so long, and so much longer than you. But I remember you, I remember the day you and your wife, this young woman who is like a daughter to me, came to this place, some belongings packed on the back of a mule, and some carried on your own backs. The mute boy, Qasim, was a baby and you carried him as if he was the most precious thing you had. And indeed he is precious, he is life, and he will beget life, sons who will defend our land from the infidel.

I was already here for many years, before the English doctor and the German one and even this last one, the one who died in that basement. What was his name, son? What did we call him, those of us who could still remember to talk with words, not animal sounds?

Daud Ali Shah. Yes, I remember, that was his name. Or that is what we knew him as. They say he refused to leave us all behind after that first raid, so he pleaded with the rebels to spare him, to let him take care of us. The others fled, or were killed. The women—of course, you know what happened to the women. We shall not talk about that, my son. We shall not dishonor our daughters by speaking of what happened to them.

Yes, that Firangi Doctor—he died for us in that basement down there. The rebels said they would keep him for ransom, so they took him downstairs and locked him up. Even you, Waris, even you could not help him. It was too late by the time you managed to break the lock on that basement door. He was already dead, strangled by a rope he had used to hang himself. May God keep his soul, even if it is a sin to take one's own life.

But what is not a sin, my son? When is a death not a sin? And when is a death a righteous thing, a just thing? Only when God wills it, my son. And in this case, I do not believe that Allah wanted this man to die, as much as he has not wanted any of these people here to die, these men frail of body and mind, these children who have no one to call their own, and me, foolish old man who lost everything and then found everything when I came here, all those years ago. So many years ago.

I am now a hundred years old, maybe even older. God knows—my mother could not read or write, nor could anyone else in the family except the mullah who recited the azaan in my ears the day I was born, bringing me into the faith. But I do remember that when I was a very young child there was another war, and then another one, and several more throughout the time I was growing up. My father, God bless his soul, my father was a simple man, like most folk in our village up in the mountains of Kunarbagh. When the Firangi sent its army to conquer our land, my father joined the lashkar of forces that fought this foreign army, sending them back to Hindustan from where they had come.

But those are other stories. Those stories I will tell you when you have the time to listen. I do not want to burden you with all that I *know, all that these sinful eyes have seen. Of course, now I do not see so well, but these eyes can still tell good from evil and I can tell you that the Firangi has always had evil designs on our land, they have always wanted to conquer us. But God made us a proud people, and we did not allow strangers to come and take our land and our women and our honor away from us. I do not know who these foreigners are this time—if they are the sons of the same ones who came a hundred years ago when I was a boy, or if this is a different breed. All I know is that they have come to destroy our land and take away all that is precious to us. All I know is that we must fight them, and we must protect what is ours—our land, our women, our honor.*

Noor Kaka spoke till we had almost fallen asleep. I still don't know who he is, what he was doing in this asylum, where he had come from. But perhaps that will come later, on some other night when we gather again to hear his story. He has obviously not seen that I too am a Firangi, the son of those who came a hundred years ago to take away all he had. I don't know if that is because he is too old and frail and his glasses are broken, or because it is so dark in the kitchen that he cannot make out that I am different.

Actually, I'm not too sure about that anymore. I haven't shaved since I was locked up here, I haven't bathed, I haven't had a change of clothes, and I wear an old curtain around my shoulders, the shawl given to me by Waris now covering Noor Kaka's bony body. I haven't seen myself in a mirror in a long time, and it is quite possible that there is not much difference now between me and these people here.

Bulbul has brought me a small mirror. It is almost as if

this young man is clairvoyant, as if he read my mind last night in the smoke-filled kitchen where you can't see the back of your own hand even if you hold it up next to your nose.

The mirror is embedded in the round tin box that holds his treasures. He keeps this box in the pocket of his jeans. He had shown me the picture of the actress in the Rexine boots once, and offered the snuff wrapped up in cigarette foil on another occasion. But this time he has some more things to show me, gathered from the debris and from the pockets of the men we buried the day after the bombing.

These are strange things, bizarre bits of people's lives gleaned from a harvest of ruin. There is a gold molar, a silver ring with a large rust-colored stone, a broken comb, a silver amulet, a plastic wallet, some dog-eared photographs, and a walnut. Bulbul takes these items and shows them to me as if they are prizes he won in a school sporting event, winning the three-legged race in the courtyard of this damned place. He sets each one in the palm of his extended hand and admires it before passing it to me, narrowing his eyes and assessing the merits of the piece. He talks about the items with great zest, extolling their virtues, selling their charms. I am amused by this, but I also see that for Bulbul this is not just a game—he is offering me some of these treasures not as gifts, but in exchange for the things he has asked for, the hiking boots and orange parka and yellow corduroys that he saw in the Sears catalog. I cannot believe that he still remembers that ridiculous request, I cannot believe it after all that has happened, the deaths and the assaults and the bombing. I cannot believe that this man

is still convinced that I will get out of here and send him
the things he desires so deeply.

I know I can't tell him otherwise, and perhaps it is
necessary for me, too, to believe that I will get out. That
is the only thought which keeps me going, which keeps
me from wanting to take the same route that Dr. David
Elisha did, or Daud Ali Shah as Noor Kaka chose to describe him. But I think that in order to take my own life I
will need much more courage than I have, and whatever
courage I do have, I need to survive this.

As it is, the basement where I could carry out my
own hanging is filled with the ill and the insane. I have
not been down there since the bombing, but I believe
the place reeks like a toilet, that there are rivers of urine
everywhere, and that those who were sick have become
moreso now, locked up without the sun, waiting for the
next attack or death, whichever comes first.

I have taken the comb from Bulbul's box of treasures. I
asked him whether he would let me borrow the mirror in
order to check what I look like after all this time. I have
become haggard and pale, there are dark circles around
my eyes, and scabs where I have scratched myself, where
invisible creatures have bitten me and sucked my blood.
My hair is like thatch, dry and standing on top of my
head like a sheaf of wheat. I try to use the comb on my
hair—its teeth stick to the dirt and become entangled in
the knots. Bulbul leaves me for a while with the mirror,
while I struggle to come to terms with the stranger staring back at me. When Bulbul returns he holds a mug of
water in one hand and a bottle of mustard-seed oil in the
other. He tells me I should dip the comb in the water,

it will make the task of taming my hair easier. I do so, and once the knots have been unraveled, Bulbul pours a bit of the oil on his palm and rubs his hands together. Then he applies the oil to my hair, massaging my scalp gently. I am concerned at this proximity—I have never really known how to respond to what I consider to be Bulbul's overtures. But the massage and his tenderness overwhelm me. I let him do what he is doing, close my eyes, and lean against the wall of my cell. I could not have imagined letting a man touch me, let alone run his fingers through my hair. But then I could not have imagined most of the things that have happened here, and sometimes we fear things only because we do not know them, like the touch of a man's hand against your own skin.

I must have fallen asleep at some point. When I awoke, I was still leaning against the stone wall of my cell. The sun was traveling rapidly in its journey beyond the mountains. It left patches of light on the walls and then moved on quickly. I felt a fleeting blaze of warmth as the sun settled on me for a brief moment. I felt well, and I knew that I was now closer to leaving this desolate place than I had ever been.

Bulbul asked me for the mirror when we met in the kitchen this evening. He smiled shyly and said that he wanted to wash and clean and comb his hair so that he could be ready for Anarguli when she came to join us for the meal. Noor Jehan has declared that Anarguli and Hayat cannot be left in the basement with the others—it is not right, it is not healthy for either the girl or the old woman. No one objects to this, although it is not usual for women to eat in the company of men. We have only known Noor Jehan among us, and she is like a mother, so those rules do not apply to her. But Ánarguli is still a young girl, beautiful, with no husband or father or son to protect her, so she must be given separate quarters. At least this is what I am told by Sabir, who laughs while telling me, winking with his one good eye and suggesting that even in this madness there are rules to follow, a code of honor to live by.

Only the kitchen, my cell, which must have been an outhouse, and one other room, possibly a garage at some time (it only has three walls), stand in this forlorn compound. The rest of the buildings have been wrecked. In places only walls stand, as if they are waiting for someone to reclaim them and reassign some sort of purpose to their existence. These walls are as scarred and pitted as Sabir's face and they seem to have witnessed the same horrors as him. Sabir says the animals will sleep in that garage when it begins to snow. We have to start looking for food again for the animals, and for us, and for the men breathing the foul air of their underground vault.

Waris says we must find a way to cordon off the area where the unexploded bomb lies stuck in the debris. He does not want any of the men in the basement to wander around and come across it, setting it off, helping it to destroy its target of a handful of madmen, starved and filthy and completely ignorant of the death that awaits them.

Sabir came to me today for the first time. He was awkward, this man of unwavering courage. He stood outside the cell leaning on his crutch, a mug of tea in his hand. He called out to me and then said, politely, in English: *What is your good name? Please tell to me.*

I thought I must be hearing things—I had gotten so used to Bulbul's brand of communication which was largely an amalgam of several European languages picked up from tourists on Chicken Street. This was the first time I had heard a complete English sentence, co-herent, even if a bit quaint. I got up to meet him and shook his hand. He offered me the mug of tea and asked me to sit with him beneath the tree in the middle of the courtyard. I followed him, wondering what this invita-tion was going to lead to. Another scheme to look for food, another plan to gather supplies from the valley of the dead?

Sabir waited for a while before speaking and I sipped the hot tea, letting the liquid warm my insides and the enamel mug warm my fingers. It had snowed on the mountains again—I could tell from the chill in the air, it's the same at home when the Sierra Nevada receives its first snowfall of winter.

Before Sabir began to speak he dug into his shirt pocket and brought out a fountain pen. It was not expen-sive, but it had ink in its cartridge and it worked. This I could see when Sabir pulled out a small diary from the same pocket and began to write something in his own language. He spoke the words as he wrote; I have heard them often in this country: *Bismillah al Rahman al Rahim, In the Name of God the Merciful.* Then he held the diary in his hands and offered it to me.

Write your name here. Tell to me where you are coming from, who is being in your family, what you may be doing in this country.

I wasn't sure why he was asking me to do all this. His tone of voice was not belligerent, but I sensed more than cursory curiosity. What am I doing in this country? I wanted to say. He could see for himself what I'm doing in his goddamned country, but I held my tongue in check and wrote my name on the opened page of his diary. He took it from me, then faced me as he spoke, clearly and with purpose.

My brother, you may be thinking that none of us here has any use for letters and for pens and paper. I have watched you in the kitchen as you write in your pages, and I have wanted to ask you what it is that you write. I thought that perhaps it was secret, your writing, that it was of no use to anyone except yourself.

But today I have come to ask you to write something for all of us here. I do not know how much longer we can last in this place, with not much food or clean water. Unless it rains again we will have no fresh water, and unless one of us leaves this compound in search of food, we will have nothing to eat. And of course, my brother, it will snow here soon, and none of us has any warm clothing, except the boy Bulbul who wears that foolish scarf around his neck like a woman.

In short, my brother, it seems as if the end will come quickly to this place, and it will take all of us. You have seen the bombing, and you have seen what the rebel soldiers can do. We do not have any weapons; we do not even know how long we can keep these people in that basement before they start dying from disease, or they start killing each other. All we know is that we have not been able to honor the dead of Tarasmun, and there is nothing worse for a man of dignity than to die without honor. We do not want to die like rats trapped in the basement—I will face death like a man, even though I am only half of one.

But what will happen once there is no one here to bury us? Who will know the names of the dead, who will recite the fatehah at our graves? Who will tell our loved ones that we are no more?

My brother—I was working for the government, a technician in the chemistry laboratory of the university in the city, before this war. I left the country many years ago to study; I went to the land which is supposed to be responsible for many of the problems we face today. But it was there that I learned that each human being has the ability to learn, to do good, to go forward. I was the only one in my village who went to school—I was the only one who wanted to change the way we have lived for centuries. I wanted my sisters to learn, I wanted them to know that they were worthy of respect, and were not born just to serve us men. But the mullah in the village thought I was going to make the girls turn wayward—he warned me that the little I taught my sisters would expose them to evil, that they would be able to write letters to boys, that they would learn the ways of city women who have no shame, that they would bring dishonor to our families, to the village and the tribe. I insisted that our Prophet, may Peace be Upon Him, commanded that even if we have to go to China to learn, we must go. And that meant all of us, women too. But the mullah would not understand this simple truth. He made up a story of how I had insulted the Prophet, how I had burned and destroyed our Holy Qura'an. And he made sure that I would never teach my sisters anything that would change their lives.

But, my brother, my life changed, completely and totally. I left the village to return to the city where the job I had held is not available to a man with one eye and a face that would frighten children and the faint-hearted even in daylight. I rushed back to the university, but I was too late. I not only lost my job, but also my leg and my dignity. I arrived at the university the day there was a raid on my department. Actually, a professor was getting married that day, his bride was another teacher of science, a beautiful young woman who spoke

softly and knew so much at such a young age. The ceremony was in
the grounds of the university. I got there after the rebel soldiers had
already done what they had to do. They forced the marriage party
into the chemistry lab where they tied up the bride and the profes-
sor and made them lie together in a box two meters long and one
meter wide. Then they doused the two of them with the acid in the
lab. When I found them they could not be recognized, except for the
bride's white gown, like the ones your women wear in your country.
There was a message written on a piece of paper and left on top of the
box. It said: These are the bodies of Godless Communists
who Shame our Country and Do not Follow the Faith.

I rushed out of the lab, horrified. I must have been screaming, for
one of the rebels heard me and found me, and began to shoot at me,
hitting my leg many times. Each time I fell, he would laugh. I could
not hide, I was in an open area, there was no shelter anywhere. He
shot at me until I couldn't move anymore, until my leg was severed
at the knee.

I lost my leg and my faith in humankind that day, brother. But
still I live, and I have no idea what keeps me alive. Maybe it is the
fact that even with only one leg and one eye, I still have my mind and
my memories, which is more than what most of these people here
have. Perhaps it would be better to have neither mind nor memories,
not the memories I have.

When Sabir finished his story the tea in my mug was
stone cold, and I was shivering despite the fact that the
sun had warmed the courtyard and shone above us like
a beacon.

Waris and Sabir have asked me to come with them to
the basement before we eat this evening. I am to make
a list of the people left alive in this asylum. And then

I'm supposed to list all of us on a separate page, noting down family names and villages and post office addresses. These lists will then be put in a place where they can be found by whoever chooses to come to Tarasmun once the war is over. And if none of us survive, at least we will have plaques with our names on them, marking our graves.

six

The air in the basement was thick with the stench of human waste. I choked going down the stairs and had to keep my nose and mouth covered for fear of vomiting from the nausea which almost blinded me. Waris led the way, Bulbul followed. We had to find a place where we could stand without falling over any of the men who lay across the floor like corpses. Waris hung the lantern on the wall and I stood beneath it, Sabir's diary in my hands, the pages trembling like a delirious man's mouth.

Bulbul made his way to each man and sat on his haunches, looking into his face, talking to him, asking questions to which he would seldom get an answer. Waris knew the names of most, some of who he and other members of the staff (disappeared or dead now) had named in order to identify them on the day they were washed and deloused. There were never enough supplies to be wasted or used haphazardly, and so the men's names would be written in a register each time they were tested for worms or doused. Among the men who wouldn't speak, or whose language could not be understood, was one named Geedar, since his high-pitched laughter sounded like the cry of a jackal. Bulbul sat next to Geedar and talked to him in a low voice, like a mother coaxing a child to sleep. Geedar kept looking at Bulbul, a small smile perking up his filthy face. He blinked at him, picked his teeth with his fingers, then spat a huge glob of phlegm at Bulbul's feet. Bulbul stood up in disgust; Geedar broke into his high-pitched screech and several others joined him in the yelping that filled the basement like sounds from a crypt, which in essence it was. Waris helped me fill the empty pages of the diary—we listed eighteen men and three young boys. Of these, one is very small, stunted, with a crooked back. He looks like a child except for the slight beard covering his jaw. His voice, too, is like a child's. At least he can speak and he gave Waris the name of his father and his address: *Mohammad Ayub, resident of Village Darabad, Farah Province.*

This boy's name is Karim—he is called Karim Kuchak, Karim the Small. He tells Waris his father tried to sell him and his three sisters after the war began and their village was destroyed, when there was no money with which to feed them. The shopkeepers in the area collected some money for him, telling him to keep at least the youngest one, a baby. The other two sisters were bought by someone crossing the border that day, but no one wanted him *(I am so small, you know! Karim Kuchak is my name!)*, so his father left him here, in the hope that at least he would get food and shelter. *(And now look—no food, no shelter! Karim Kuchak is hungry and cold!)*

This amazing character talked like a person possessed, and I could hardly write all that he said, but I did get his father's name which he checked to see if it was noted correctly. I handed him the diary, he looked at it very seriously, holding it upside down, then nodded and handed it back to me. He offered me his hand and I shook it, reminding me that I must wash as soon as I got out of that stinked-up hole in the ground.

* * *

I really don't think this exercise is worth anything, except that it keeps us busy and "purposefully engaged," as they would say in the real world. No one is going to find this list of people here, and even if they do, what use will it be when none of us are around to see whether our graves are marked with our names or not? No one is going to come and mourn us—at least, I don't think anyone will come all the way from the Pentagon to check up on me anytime soon.

Noor Jehan has brought Anarguli and Hayat into the kitchen, asking us to leave while she heats up a mug of water and washes the women behind a torn burlap curtain she devised this morning while we were in the basement. Sabir tells her she must be careful with the water—it seems that this year winter rains will be late, possibly because the air is choked with the dust churned up from the bombing, changing the weather pattern.

It seems a lot of things have changed this year, a lot of things will be different, and the weather is the least of them.

We were joined in the courtyard by Noor Kaka while Noor Jehan attended to the women. Waris insists that the men in the basement be brought out in small groups so that in case of an attack, it will be easier to herd them back in. The last time, so many of them died just watching the mayhem—it's possible that they had no idea what was happening around them, they just stood there as the buildings of the compound collapsed and fellow inmates were crushed to death as if it was nothing extraordinary, just another day of madness.

Noor Kaka was one of the first to be brought out. I think Waris still feels guilty about having abandoned him underneath all that rubble, and so makes up for it by extending him kindness whenever he can. This afternoon, Waris led him to the tree in the middle of the courtyard and sat him down beneath it, first laying a frayed burlap bag on the ground. Then he sat next to Noor and offered him a pinch of the tobacco that seems to keep him and Sabir going. Noor sucked on it for a while before spitting it out and speaking.

Son, you may not believe it now, seeing me in this miserable state, filthy rags for clothes, no shoes on my feet, and hardly anything to my name. But there was a time when I was a fine specimen of manhood—I was young too, Waris Khan, like you and this boy with the red scarf, this Bulbul, child of Ababeel, the bird who will warn us of the approach of the Day of Judgment.

Many years ago, when you were not even born—when we still had our pride and when kings ruled our country—I stood alongside my father and defended this land from those who came to rob us of what was ours. There had already been many wars before the one I fought in—my father would tell us the tales, and his father before that. I grew up wanting to be like them so I memorized their stories, and now those stories are etched deep in my heart.

The first war which my grandfather fought was in the year 1842. It was winter, icy winds blew straight down from the distant peaks of the Hindu Kush. They howled as they traveled across the snow-covered wasteland where a handful of desperate, frozen men staggered down the boulder-strewn tracks leading to the few hovels of our village. A week before there had been 4,000 of them—700 Brit-

ish soldiers and the rest Indian sepoys. The previous evening they had numbered only a hundred or so. Now, after a fearful night of fighting and panic in the freezing twists and turns of a narrow pass, there were barely forty men on their feet, of who only half were in any condition to fight. The Indian troops were long gone, killed, frozen to death, or lost forever in the grim mountains. Only the British remained, some officers of various regiments.

My grandfather told me that he had waited at the end of the pass to finish off those men, those invaders of our country. Across the land there was nothing but anger at how the Firangi had butchered our men, women, and even children. There was little food or fuel to sustain our troops, and the weapons we had were muskets and long knives with which we could rush in and stab the invader, slashing them till we were sure there were no more waiting to loot our land.

These men, the Firangi, they wore brilliant uniforms, yellow-faced coatees and white cross-belts, with long greatcoats that did not do much to protect them from the bitter cold. We had little to keep us warm, except the fervor of our loyalty. A few of our men had posteens from the sheep we would slaughter for food, but often there would be no footwear except for the strips of leather the men would bind around their feet. Many soldiers lost their feet to the snow and ice, but they did not lose their passion for the battle which had to be won.

We watched the Firangi as they struggled through the pass, their hands frozen and fingers unable to load their heavy muskets. Their ranks had thinned and we were amazed at their insistence on carrying on what was already a lost battle. We waited until they were close enough for us to see the fear and fatigue in their eyes, and then we came down the side of that mountain to claim the enemy as ours. They did not even have time to draw their swords or fix their bayonets into their muskets.

My grandfather and several of the elder men were on horseback—

when the Firangi were surrounded, my grandfather let out a cry that pierced the ice and cracked it like a giant boulder. The Firangi were crouching in a crevice, waiting for the worst, but my grandfather did not fire at them—he rode up to them and offered his hand in friendship. He told them that if they handed over their arms, all would be well for them.

One man came forward to meet my grandfather. He wore medals on his chest and a brilliant waistband, and announced that he was Captain Souter of Her Majesty's 44th Regiment of Foot. He stood before my grandfather and declared that he would rather die than give up his arms. My grandfather tried to reason with him, reminding him that death was the only certainty for him and his troops. It was better to do as asked and to save themselves from further bloodshed.

This Firangi officer, he was a bold one, an admirable one, fearless. He stepped up to my grandfather and grabbed his musket. At this, the men following my grandfather began to shoot, and suddenly the rest of our men waiting on the neighboring hilltop rushed down to settle the argument. Our men were armed with long-barreled jezails, guns that had a longer range and better accuracy than the arms held by the Firangi. Most of Souter's men were killed; six were taken captive, among them the captain himself. Later, when he was searched, it was discovered that he had collected the bayonets of the fallen men and hidden them in his belt. He was certainly a brave one, that man, worthy of anyone's respect. My grandfather described him to me, a tall man with yellow hair—he preferred to call him Kaptan Shutar, Captain Camel.

We have great regard for those who die fighting, but Souter's courage was nothing compared to the passion of our men who stood triumphantly over the hills of Gandamak, proud of having defeated the enemy, the unwanted Firangi.

Dusk had fallen by the time Noor Kaka finished his story.

Cold winds had started blowing through the narrow passes in the mountains and I wondered whether Captain Souter's bones were buried anywhere near here, like mine will be, in the hard remorseless soil of this land. At least he died fighting—I will probably just die like a rat in a basement, drowned in the urine of a dozen insane men.

The curtain I wear to keep myself warm is not going to do me any good for much longer. I want to ask Waris to let me stay in the kitchen where he and his family and Sabir and Bulbul also sleep. I want the warmth of the kitchen, and I want to know that there are others here, that I am not alone, fighting on so many fronts.

I entered the kitchen with the intention of speaking earnestly to Sabir, who would then ask Waris to let me stay. I would take up just a corner of the room and leave in the morning, spending the day in the courtyard. As it was, I really didn't know how much longer any of us had—supplies had dwindled, the rebels could return anytime, and the bombers, they could reappear like spirits out of the sky without any warning at all.

In the kitchen I was surprised to see something quite unexpected. Noor Jehan sat before the hearth stirring a large cauldron of gruel. Next to her sat Hayat, holding a knife in her hand with which she peeled potatoes. And in the corner sat Anarguli, beautiful, troubled Anarguli, her face averted but her skin glowing in the soft light of the cooking fire. In her hands she held a pestle which she pounded rhythmically into a mortar, beating rock salt into a fine dust.

None of what I saw betrayed the chaos we had seen

below in the basement, or outside in the compound, with the bombed-out building and the bullet-scarred walls. I am constantly amazed at how these people manage to carry on as if nothing has happened, nothing out of the ordinary. Perhaps this is as ordinary as it gets here; many of the younger ones were born in war and have known nothing else.

Bulbul appeared shortly after me. I smelled him before I saw him—he must have splashed on some of that lice-killing lotion, and he had preened himself like a baboon in mating season. His hair was slicked down and he wore a hat he must have found in the ruins—it was an old tweed cap, the kind a golfer would wear on a Sunday morning. I wonder whose it could have been—the Canadian doctor's, perhaps? Were there any golf courses here before the war?

Bulbul winked at me as soon as he saw me, then pointed with his chin to the corner where Anarguli sat, engrossed in preparing the spices for the evening's meal. She held some dried red pepper in her hand and was breaking off the brittle stalks one by one. Bulbul walked toward her softly and sat beside her. Noor Jehan turned to look at him. She smiled. I watched as he took the red pepper from Anarguli's hand and began to break it into smaller pieces, adding it to the stone mortar. He was saying something to her; I couldn't hear him, but I saw him taking her hands and wiping them with the end of his scarf. Then he pointed his fingers toward his eyes, and I realized he was telling her that she must not get the dangerous seeds of the red pepper in her eyes. I had no idea whether she could see him, but I knew she understood him, and even from the distance of my corner,

I saw her smiling at Bulbul, her face still averted but her heart open to the love he wanted to offer her.

When Sabir came I asked him to speak to Waris about letting me sleep in the kitchen. Sabir patted me on the back and laughed, telling me: *My brother, is that something you have to ask us? You are our guest, a mehmaan, we must give you the best place in the house. And if there is no suitable place for such a revered guest as you, then we must find it in our hearts!*

I have to grant this much to Sabir—he knows how to spin my head around faster than a roller coaster in the Magic Kingdom. The best place in the house, tell me about it.

All of them have fallen asleep. Waris has made a small place for Noor Kaka so now there are nine of us in the kitchen. Maybe the warmth of our bodies will keep the cold out once the fire dies down.

Hayat snores gently near the hearth. She sleeps with the knife grasped in her hand. I can barely see the tattoos Bulbul mentioned—it seems as if dark shadows mark her arms, patterns of waves undulating on her flesh. Perhaps I am imagining this. Perhaps it is just the shadows cast by the dying fire, but I can see that she has a dark stain around her lips which makes her mouth look like it has been embroidered. The shape of the stain is like a man's mustache, and I wonder if this is something that was done to her by people to beautify her, or whether it is a birthmark. Or if my mind is slowly losing its grip on reality.

It is so quiet here at this time, once the day's monotonous chores have been done. All I do is wait and count the hours till salvation. It is hard to imagine that a week ago the compound resounded with so much ear-splitting noise during the bombing. All I can hear now is the sound of deep, regular breathing, an occasional murmur, and crickets that sing their dirge from some recess hidden in the depths of this place.

Bulbul talks softly in his sleep. I cannot catch what he says. Waris has insisted that he sleep across the room from Anarguli. Noor Kaka sleeps next to Anarguli, his head resting on Sabir's crutch. Noor Jehan cradles Qasim close to her and Waris sleeps near the door, his feet sprawled out across the entrance. He keeps his shoes on even while sleeping, ready for anything that might happen at any time.

I have been given the place of honor nearest the fire. I share it with Hayat, also an outsider of unknown origin, with a story that I still have to hear.

It is dark. I cannot sleep, not even in the relative comfort of the kitchen. I stare at the darkness, at the shapeless forms around me, moving gently with the breath that enters them and sustains them in this time of so much uncertainty. I watch them, and I watch the darkness hoping that it will reveal what I need to know most.

Hayat is awake too. She sits with the knife clasped in her hand and observes me as if she has known me for a while. Then she moves toward me—the knife catches some light from the glow in the hearth and throws a flash of red in my direction. I don't move, I don't know what she will do next, and I don't want to be butchered here, on the kitchen floor, by a woman who has more hair on her body than all the men in Tarasmun.

Hayat sidles toward me. She comes close enough for

me to see the intricate lines etched around her mouth. I can also see the gray hairs of her beard and the deep sockets of her eyes. I am as fascinated as I am afraid. Who is this creature who has come from a land even stranger than this one? A land which produces women who grow beards and are marked like snakes?

Hayat shoves her face forward. I can smell her breath and I gag. She is breathing hard, as if slithering along the floor with that knife in her hand has exhausted her. She stares at me and then reaches inside her tattered robe. In one sudden move she rips off an amulet strung on a grimy, beaded string. She bows her head, closing her eyes.

I have frozen into a numb carcass. She prods my shoulder with the point of her knife and I retreat further into my corner. No one moves in the dark stillness. She whispers something I do not understand. Then she hands me the amulet. I take it only because of the fear slinking down my back. It takes me awhile to gather myself and open my clenched fist which holds the amulet. My fingers unfurl like a leaf and I hold it tentatively, examining it in the embers of the fire. It is a metal disc engraved with elaborate markings. I lean forward, holding it closer to the fire. There is a design etched into the metal, three fish following each other in a circle. There are wavy lines surrounding that circle, like the ocean, and jagged lines which could be mountain peaks.

I look back at Hayat. She has opened her eyes and stares at me. I question her with my hands, she moves closer to me and whispers something in my ear. I am not sure what she says, it sounds like short bursts of staccato fire: *Ainu, Shiraoi, Iburi*. I gaze at the disc as if it could decipher the words for me. Hayat repeats the words: *Ainu, Shiraoi, Iburi.* I am totally lost. Then she speaks again and I believe I recognize one of the words, unless I have totally lost my mind. She snatches the amulet back from me and spits out the words: *Ainu, Shiraoi, Iburi, Bihoro, Katami, Honbetsuy, Tokachi, Kusharo, Kushiro, Kurile, Kurile, Kurilskaya.*

She says these words rapidly, then repeats the last one over and over again, pointing to the disc with the fish and the mountains on it: *Kurile, Kurile, Kurile.*

Could she be talking about the Kurile Islands near Japan? Could this crazed woman be a native of those islands which were surrendered to Japan by Russia more than a hundred years ago? How old is this woman, and how on earth did she get here from that place thousands of miles away?

I do not believe this and close my eyes, wanting to shut out the night and the confusion. I can still hear her breathing, repeating the same words: *Ainu, Ainu, Ainu.*

This morning I thought I should make one last effort to secure my release from this place of madness. Now that I am no longer stuck in that cell I believe I have an opportunity to escape from here, and even if I don't get very far at least I will have tried and died fighting, like Captain Souter, the Camel Man dressed in yellow and convinced of the rightness of his mission of conquest.

But I've never wanted to conquer anything. All I wanted was to find a reason for my sister which would help her understand her husband's death. All I have found so far is the absolute madness of war, and all I want now is to get as far away from this madness as I can.

* * *

I talked to Bulbul this afternoon after spending the morning wandering around the compound, searching for something that would lead me toward an exit. I know all ways out of here are blocked—the massive gate which protected this place collapsed and blocked the entrance in one of the earlier strikes, when the warlords used rocket launchers collected over years of warfare. The unexploded bomb sits in front of that gate like a treacherous guardian who will betray you the minute you approach. The only place left in and out of this god-forsaken place was the hole in the wall which has now been repaired, thanks to the diligence of Waris and his crew, and to my stupidity. Why hadn't I left when there was an opportunity to do so? Probably because Waris watches me with hawk eyes, and I didn't have any idea where I would go, dressed in a curtain and a dead man's clothes.

I still don't know where I will go if I get out of here. The rebels took the jeep when they captured me, and there's not much chance I will get far on foot.

Bulbul was buoyant when I sought him out, basking in the warmth of having seen Anarguli and spent time with her in the kitchen. She and Hayat were brought out into the courtyard, and were seated beneath the tree near the well. Hayat held the same knife in her hand; she was ripping off the skin from a dead twig and gnawing it, supplementing her diet, obviously. She would chew and spit a glob of greenish fiber into the palm of her hand, smell it, then wipe it with that amulet she had shown me.

When she saw me, she acknowledged my presence by bowing her head and closing her eyes. I nodded back at her, then surveyed the courtyard before I spoke to Bulbul about my planned "departure." Waris had brought out six men from the basement; six others had been taken out in the morning and guided to a pit in the corner which is being used as a toilet. I gag every time I have to go, and the odor of the excrement clings to my already filthy clothes like a really bad memory. Bulbul laughed the first time he saw me heaving near that nasty open pit. He patted me on the back and said: *Hey, Firangi, here we treat shit like shit!*

Waris was busy digging another pit along the side of the wall. I don't know what purpose another hole in the ground will fulfill, but at least it kept him occupied so he wouldn't listen in on my conversation with Bulbul, animated as it has to be since the language of words is not sufficient for my half-crazed friend.

I sat beside Bulbul and cleared my throat to begin the speech I rehearsed in my head last night. I told him it was time I found a way to leave this place since my family would be worried sick. In any case, the rebels were probably not coming back, food is scarce, and one less person would mean that the others would have more to eat.

Bulbul looked up at me and let a manic grin spread slowly across his face like a river in flood. I prepared myself for the worst—that he would begin laughing and draw attention to us sitting together. That would be the end of any attempt on my part to confide in him.

He laughed. Loudly. I wanted to kill myself for even bothering to talk to him. He was just like the others, like Geedar with his hyena screech and Karim Kuchak with his refrain of *Look at me, I am so small!* I shouldn't have talked to him, but who can I speak to about my plans to get out? How can I do this alone?

I worried about Waris hearing Bulbul's manic outburst but he was engrossed in digging, and only Anarguli and Hayat looked toward us. Bulbul saw Anarguli and waved to her; she actually lifted her hand and made a small gesture of acknowledgment. She could see, it seemed. Perhaps it was the dark which made her blind. Night blindness, caused by a vitamin deficiency? That must be it, I thought, when Bulbul started babbling in his strange tongue: *My friend, you think the food you eat takes away our share from us? Is that what you think?*

I nodded, convinced of the rightness of my argument. He laughed again, then bent down to the ground and picked up a pebble. He held the pebble in the palm of his hand and looked at it as if it were a gem, a precious jewel, admiring it with his monkey eyes. Then he reached for my hand and placed the pebble in my palm.

Each one of us is born with our names written on grains of wheat that Allah has provided for us, my friend. You have your share, I have mine, they have theirs. No one is hungry here; we all have what we are meant to have.

Yeah, sure, I thought to myself. That's why the woman you love probably can't see at night—because she had her share of wheat when she needed it. And Karim Kuchak had his in order to become the stunted little dwarf that he is, and Geedar with the manic screech has a brain the size of a pea because he got *his* share of wheat with his name written on it.

It is impossible to talk to these people. There's no logic here at all—everything is nonsense strung together like lines from a bad poem. I wanted to tell him that

I am hungry all the time, I am sick of the gruel Noor Jehan cooks up for us even if she tries to make it more palatable with the spices from the basement. I wanted to tell him this is not the way I'm supposed to live my life, that I don't want to end it like this either, in a dead man's clothes with nothing but a large gaping hole in my belly.

But I couldn't have said much, for just as I was trying to find the words, Anarguli screamed and fell onto the ground beneath the tree. Hayat was hunched up behind her, holding the knife which was now tipped with blood and gleamed in the sunlight.

We have revived Anarguli; she rests in the kitchen, protected and cared for by Noor Jehan and Sabir. She hadn't actually passed out; she was just hysterical and probably frightened to death of what Hayat was trying to do to her. When Bulbul and I rushed to Anarguli, Waris ran across the courtyard, shovel in hand, and almost hit Hayat with it, believing she was harming Anarguli with that knife. But Bulbul seemed to know better—he held on to Anarguli and asked me to restrain Hayat, to try to get the knife away from her.

I held Hayat's arms behind her back in the manner that we were trained at boot camp. She did not resist, she just kept making some whistling sounds like air being expelled from a punctured tire. Anarguli was swooning and Bulbul called out to Noor Jehan. She hurried from the kitchen and helped him carry Anarguli inside. Waris and I held Hayat and dragged her to the room where the animals were gathered for the night. She kept looking at me and showing me the amulet again. It was now covered with that green spittle, and it made me sick to look at it.

Once we were inside the shed, Hayat tore her bodice open from the back and pulled it down to show us several markings between her shoulder blades. These were tattoos in the shape of swastikas the color of ash, etched deep into her skin. Waris turned away; I kept looking, trying to decipher what this meant, the swastikas, her amulet, the knife with which she wanted to cut Anarguli.

Hayat began blabbering again, in a mix of the local language and the one in which she had spoken to me last night. Waris asked me to hold on to her while he went to search for Sabir. I dragged her to a corner of the shed and did what I could never have imagined I would do to a woman—I pulled her ridiculous braid out from under her veil and tied it to a stake in the ground. This is where we tied the camel and mule to keep them from straying in the night. I was confused by the power I was exercising over this lost, insane woman who had dared to trust me, and I was terrified that I was becoming like those I have always detested, the ones who would inflict cruelty on those who can't strike back. Maybe it's this place that is making me do things I don't want to. Maybe that is what makes people behave the way they do—the place they find themselves in, the place which shows them what is good, what is evil, and what is necessary. Maybe that place is always inside us, waiting to be entered.

Sabir hobbled into the shed and went straight to Hayat, who began talking the moment she saw him. He translated her speech to me after she had exhausted herself and slumped onto the straw-covered floor.

She told him that she was a healer, an Ainu woman from the island of Kurile near Japan. Her father, Miyamoto, a famous healer himself, was the chief of their tribe in Iburi province. She was his oldest daughter and had been taught how to heal illness and injury. She had also been taught the traditional practice of carving tattoos into the arms and faces of the men and women of her tribe. But it was the healing that gave her power; it was the healing that Haji Allum wanted to learn from her, to take back to his people beyond those mountains outside this asylum.

We listened in amazement to this woman's story. Sabir struggled to keep up with her staccato rhythm and total absence of pauses between thoughts.

My father, the great Miyamoto, was taken away by the Japanese from the island of Shumushu to the mainland. My family was promised protection from the Russians, and we were to get Japanese papers which would let us stay on the mainland. We were first put in a place called Bettopo on the western coast of Shumushu Island. But there was not enough for us to eat—we were no longer able to hunt and fish as we had done for hundreds of years. The Japanese moved us again to Shikotan Island, where many of us died from the great fever that ate our insides and made the blood from our stomachs come out of our mouths. There were only a few houses left when the Japanese took us again and sent us on a long journey across the seas, where my father, the great chief Miyamoto, had to earn a living by carrying provisions for the men building the great line that would run through this new country, this country where there were people darker than us, but with less hair and no tattoos. There were white men there too, and people like you, Crippled One, people like him, the Gatekeeper, and like that other one who loves that girl with no hair on her head. Those people spoke your language, and they had also come from far, across another ocean, and they had brought with them many camels like the one you have standing outside, that miserable beast who smells and shows his teeth and whose arrogance is strung across his eyelashes like washing on a line.

The man who brought me here, to this desert, Haji Allum, spoke like you—he was older, like my father, and like my father he too was a healer and a collector of herbs. Haji Allum was a rich man—he had many camels, and the white people paid him well for his services. My father had nothing, we lost everything, and he once asked Haji Allum to let him have some money so he could buy clothes for us, my mother and my sisters. We had come in what we wear in Shumushu, robes we call attushi, woven from the inner bark of the mountain elm tree. We would embroider these with delicate patterns, like the tattoos we embroider on our skins. But these robes were too heavy for the desert where we found ourselves, and my father wanted us to look like the others, wearing white people's clothes.

Haji Allum gave my father money in exchange for learning the secret of healing. After many years, when I had grown up and my father had died, leaving my mother and my sisters on our own, Haji Allum offered to marry me, and my mother gave me to him believing that he would keep me safe from harm in that strange land.

Haji Allum was good to me. We traveled from that desert to this desert on a big ship, and that is where he got the great fever, bringing up blood from his stomach every night until he had no blood left. By the time we got to his village in these black mountains, Haji Allum was only bones covered with a long beard. I tried to heal him, but I did not have the herbs I needed on that ship—there was nothing there with which I could heal him, and so Haji Allum died very soon after we reached his home.

I could not heal that good man, but I know I have the power to heal this girl with the wound on her head. That tree beneath which *you sit and enjoy the air, that tree has medicine in its leaves and in its skin. We healers know this, and I know that it will cleanse the girl of the poison in her blood which is making that wound worse, even though the Gatekeeper's wife keeps washing it to keep it clean. But that is not enough—the girl needs me, she needs the power of my healing, and you have all prevented me from helping her. See, all I had to do was make the same marks that were made on my back near the base of her skull—that would heal the wound and make her well, and even make her see and speak. I have not heard the girl's voice until today, you know. At least you can believe that I have healed her voice.*

Hayat spoke without taking a breath, as if she had waited all these years to tell her story. And we listened as if we had waited all this time to hear it, this incredible tale of lost people finding others who had also gone astray.

She asked me to return her knife to her. I looked at Waris and Sabir. They said nothing and I, ashamed, lowered my head and hoped she would not hate me for having tied her up like an animal.

I don't know if I should let her have the knife. Perhaps it is better that I keep it and use it when the time comes.

seven

I still haven't had a chance to talk to Bulbul about my plan. I don't even have a plan, just a desperate desire to get out. Sometimes I feel I'm losing my mind, I don't know what is real anymore, and I don't know if what I feel is real. It's like living inside a person with several lives, none of which has any connection with the other. Sometimes I feel I have no relationship with anything, not even with the people at home who have even less of an idea what this war is all about. It's as if my heart is so still with fear that it has forgotten to beat life's rhythm into my veins.

The nails on my fingers and toes have grown until they've begun to curl like the roots of an old tree.

Sabir insists on speaking to me. I pretend he isn't there, I don't want to hear what he has to say. And I have nothing to say to him.

Bulbul, too, comes to me in my corner and keeps offering me this pale liquid they call tea.

I have large red splotches all over my back. I spend the night scratching myself like a demented man. I have been given the gift of Tarasmun in plentitude—fleabites the size of quarters, swollen and burning and driving me insane.

* * *

I must have slept last night. I traveled in my sleep, I found many graves in which small children were sleeping, curled up, their hands beneath their cheeks. When I peered inside, one of them opened his eyes and stared back at me. He was saying something but I couldn't understand the words. In his eyes I saw a reflection of myself, and in my eyes I saw a reflection of the child looking at me. There were many of us, of me and the child, of dead children and a half-crazed young man wandering into their graves.

There was a dog in the next grave, eating the foot of one of the children. He snarled and snapped at me when I came close. His mouth was bloody, his tongue marked with a swastika.

Row upon row of graves, dead children, and a dog with a bloody tongue.

There are more people sleeping in the kitchen now. Every time one of the men downstairs gets sick he is brought into the kitchen for warmth. We now have twelve people here, including a man with a very large head and stick-out ears, another with a very sallow face and a pinched nose, like a ferret, and a younger man with gangrene eating into his feet.

The big-headed man has a fever. He moans constantly, and fixes onto anyone near him, mumbling something about pomegranates and goat's milk. Noor Jehan does her best to feed him but he cannot keep anything down, and the place stinks with the stench of vomit.

The pinched man coughs the whole night long and spits up blood. I am quite sure he has tuberculosis, and I am even more sure that by the end of all this, if I do not die with a bullet in my head or a knife in my heart, I will die with blood coming out of my mouth.

The young man has auburn hair and freckles. His eyes are dark; he broods and does not speak much. He needs to be helped out every morning so that he can sit in the sun. Waris insists that he must keep his feet uncovered, exposing the rotting flesh to the air. I can almost see the bone of his ankle, or perhaps I am just imagining things, like the children in the graves who tried to talk to me, and the swastika on that dog's tongue.

Noor Jehan is having a difficult time finding a place for Anarguli and Hayat. She insists that they must have a separate space and suggests that, at least at night, the women sleep behind the burlap curtain she set up earlier. The pinched man coughs up a clot of blood and spits it into a tin can provided by Bulbul. He looks at Noor Jehan and spits again, telling her that it's too late for her to try to give these women a place of their own—it's too late for all of us. *No one knows which is outside and which is inside, sister. No one knows which is the earth and which the sky.*

The pinched man reaches into his pocket and brings out a book with a dog-eared cover, red with gold printing along the spine. He handles it carefully, reverently, as if it were a sleeping child he does not wish to wake. He opens the book and begins to recite, rocking back and forth gently and in rhythm. I hear the rounded vowels of Persian and the cadence of poetry as he reads:

Because love's sun has abandoned
The field of my heart,
The darkened landscape

Now yields only sorrow . . .

He looks up abruptly at Noor Jehan and asks her if she likes this composition, and if she does, should he sing to her, softly, like a lullaby?

Noor Jehan does not answer him but I can see that she wants to speak. She puts her hand to her mouth instead, and cups her lips as if she's trying to keep the words in. Then she quickly turns away and throws down the curtain which separates the women from us.

I don't know what troubles her, other than the obvious fact that there is certainly not enough food to go around, that disease is now rampant in this wretched compound, and that she must be tired and weary and wondering when it will all end.

Last night Sabir woke me up. I must have had another nightmare—I did not recognize him for a moment, and was afraid of him standing over me with his crutch held like a weapon. In my dream I was in a small grave again, and I was trying to put together the limbs of a child who lay on his back, looking at me, a torso and a head with dark eyes. I couldn't see the dog in the dream but I felt him, and I knew he was there, breathing his foul breath over me and the child.

When Sabir shook my shoulder, I was trying to grab the child's foot out of the mouth of the dog. I pulled at the foot and fell back into the grave. The ground beneath me was soft and wet and when I raised myself to peer out of the hole, I saw myself staring back.

Bulbul tells me this morning that I was crying in my

sleep, that Sabir had woken up and heard me, and had wanted to rouse me so that I could lose the terrible things that were troubling me. I want to tell Bulbul that I cannot lose these things, that I cannot stop seeing them even when I open my eyes.

I am on the U.S.S. George Washington. The commander of the 70th wing flying F-14s has just landed his thousandth sortie. He celebrates with us, and tells us that bombing the village was like having a gunfight at the O.K. Corral. We have chicken wings with barbecue sauce that evening.

The villages of Denar Kheil, Kala Khan, and Qarabagh were bombed with 1,000-pound CBU-87 cluster bombs, each containing 202 BLU-97 bomblets. A single bomblet kills anyone within a sixty-yard radius, and severely injures a person within 100 yards. The "mother bomb" explodes 300 to 400 feet above the ground, dispersing the bomblets which hurtle through the air attached to little parachutes, enabling wider reach of the ordinance. One CBU-87 spreads bombs over three football fields. The BLU-97 has three purposes: to destroy armored vehicles, to ignite fires around military targets such as munition depots, and to kill people with shrapnel fragments.

The barbecue sauce is thick and red and drips off my fingers and my tongue, and as I lick it I hear the sound of death walking softly behind me.

Noor Jehan keeps appearing by my side with a bowl of hot liquid which she tries to put into my mouth, but all I want to do is spit it out and sleep. Why don't they just leave me alone?

It is hot in here, and I cannot breathe. The big-headed man has ears which are like pancakes. I want to bite him, but he glares at me and shows me his teeth, jagged and streaked with red spittle.

Waris is trying to choke the life out of that little child, the one who was raped. I know we buried him but he is back in the kitchen again and Waris is trying to suffocate him so that he will not eat the food and take away our clothes.

It is cold here, in this huge empty room with goats hanging from the rafters by red rope tied around their necks.

Mama, why did you leave me and let me live? When we buried Carlos his bones were wet with your grief, and I wanted to be buried with him just so I could feel the comfort of your love once again.

I have no idea how long I have had this fever. Bulbul tells me that I said strange things to him, that he was afraid I had lost myself. Sabir sits with me and wipes the vomit from my mouth and Waris presses my feet, massaging my soles to get the blood flowing again. Noor Jehan and the boy Qasim sponge the fever from my forehead with the end of her veil.

I have urinated in my pants, and I smell like a dead goat.

Sabir tries to take the pen away from me; he tells me I must conserve my energy until I am better. What am I to tell him about how much energy it takes to not say the words which fill my head like rocks, hurting me and pressing down on my eyes until I can't see anything but despair?

* * *

There is a fire in the distance. People dance around it and sing. They are joyful; I can hear them. Their voices are like water, like a river, like the song of the ocean.

Noor Jehan has tried to make me drink this liquid but I cannot keep it down. Sabir has found a spoon somewhere and makes me sip the broth slowly. There is a strange smell in this room, as if something rotted and left its stench on the walls and on the floor.

They have brought me out into the sunlight. I don't know how long I was in that room with the dead goat. Bulbul sits beside me and sings some strange song in his broken voice. The girl he loves sits under the tree, and that crazy woman with the tattoos sits at a distance with Noor Jehan and the boy. The boy plays with his broken cart. I know I had to do something for him, but I cannot remember now. I cannot see the others. I cannot see the camel.

Maybe they killed him, and cooked and ate him.

Bulbul tells me I was sick with some great fever for many days. I still feel as if my body has been put through the teeth of a massive harvester, like the ones we saw on the farms in the valley.

Where are all those people? My mother, my sister, my family? Did she have the baby who Carlos will never see? Do they remember me?

Tranquility, California.

Home.

* * *

My father would tell us about the time when refugees from Oklahoma rolled into Tranquility like clouds of dust that had risen across the Great Plains, drifting west toward California. The wind that whipped up those clouds stripped tens of thousands of acres of their topsoil, leaving land and life impoverished. My father was a farming man, had been so for many generations before our land became the hunting ground for hungry men traveling in covered wagons, cutting into the Sierra for gold. He told us about how the soil in the Great Plains had been exposed by cultivation which killed the protecting grasses, powdered by protracted drought.

He told us how dust, drought, and the Depression pushed these pea farmers into our land, traveling in tin cars with anything they could carry stuffed in corners, and carried in the empty caverns of their hearts. After the drifting dust clouds drift the people, he said. Over the concrete ribbons of highway which lead out in every direction come the refugees.

Waris says we have a serious problem now. There is only one drum of water left, and no rain in sight. We will not be able to wash unless we use the water in the well that has human limbs floating in it.

The stench from the latrines Waris has dug along the wall is unbearable. Sabir says he will throw the limestone from the rubble into the trenches.

I don't know if it's the smell of excrement or the odor of fear which rests heavily on us like a long night without end. Noor Kaka tells us we must be brave and face this for we are men, and men do not know fear.

At night I want to hide inside the stinking quilt I sleep beneath and weep my fear into its putrid, rotting fabric. I hear my father's voice again and I listen, keeping my heart still.

* * *

At Fort Yuma the bridge over the Colorado marks the southeastern portal to California. Across this bridge move shiny cars of tourists, huge trucks, an occasional horse and wagon, or a Yuma Indian on horseback. And at intervals appear slow-moving cars loaded with refugees.

The refugees travel in old automobiles and light trucks, some of them homemade, frequently with trailers behind. All their worldly possessions are piled on the cars and covered with old canvas or ragged bedding, with perhaps bedsprings on top, a small iron stove on the running board, a battered trunk, lantern, and galvanized iron washtub tied on the back. Children, aunts, grandmothers, and a dog are jammed into the car, stretching its capacity incredibly. A neighbor boy sprawls on top of the loaded trailer.

Most of the refugees are in obvious distress. Clothing is sometimes neat and in good condition, particularly if the emigrants left last fall, came via Arizona, and made a little money in the cotton harvest there. I was young then, but I knew that something big was happening in the valley, that things would change now, that we were no longer the only ones who would plough the land and take from it the wealth held in its belly.

I can hear the yelling. It is Sabir, telling Waris that someone has to go in search of water before we begin killing each other. Waris tells him there is no water anywhere in this desert, where the dust has embraced us like a burial shroud.

In my fever I dreamed of the river where my father told me stories while we fished, or just lay on the grassy bank and stared at the tops of trees shading us from the sky. He was young when the pea farmers came to Tranquility, but he remembered the fear of losing his job to the new people who staked a claim to the land he and his father, and his father before him, had lived on and loved.

Tranquility, California.

"We got blowed out in Oklahoma," said the tall, lanky emigrant of old white stock, impoverished now and holding out his calloused hands as if something precious had been taken from him.

"Yes sir, born and raised in the state of Texas; farmed all my natural life. Ain't nothing there to stay for, nothing to eat. Something's very wrong," said a cotton farmer camping under eucalyptus trees in Imperial Valley.

A mother with seven children, whose husband died on the journey in Arizona, explained: "The drought come and burned it up. We'd have gone back to Oklahoma from Arizona, but there wasn't nothing to go to."

"Yeah, lots left ahead of us—no work of no kind," a wizened old man with white stubble said. He was old but he was still looking for work, and my father feared that it was his work which would serve the old man and his bewildered family.

"It seems like God has forsaken us back there in Arkansas," another woman told my father. Her children were filthy and thin, and they played with the equally filthy and thin dog as if they were at home in Arkansas waiting for Mother to call them in for supper, after which they would wash and pray to the Lord and thank Him for the Sweet Cream and Good Providence He had given them, and then sleep under the patchwork quilt Granny had made before she died in the time of the Great Hunger.

There is another argument. Bulbul tells me that Sabir and Waris fight all the time now about water and food. There is not enough for all of us, he says. Someone will get less than the others. But Waris tells him that all of us will eat an equal share—only Allah can deprive some and give to the others. Sabir tells him he can leave for the village again to look for food. Waris glances at him and then up at the sky before turning away.

It is dark outside. I have not left the kitchen since the first snow began to fall. There is little wood now, so Noor Jehan waits till it is time to cook and then lights the fire in the hearth. What will happen when there is nothing left to cook, and what will happen when there is no fuel to burn?

My father was not a tall man, but built well, with strong shoulders and thick, muscular arms. He married a white woman and I got her hair and her eyes. My sister got his dark color, and in school no one really believed I was the son of a Wuksachi Indian, born in the shadow of the sequoia tree. No one really believed that any of us existed anymore, and I was always listening for the sounds of his stories even after he died, for he remembered how it happened, how the land was taken away, how people of many colors came to live in Tranquility.

He told me about the black travelers from Mississippi who entered California at Fort Yuma in March, telling him that they had "just beat the water out by a quarter of a mile." A sharecropper, stopping tentless by the highway near Bakersfield, with only green onions as food for his wife and children, had tried to buy a farm in Oklahoma and lost it. But he announced proudly that he had left Wagner County "clear," owing no one. He spoke of crop restriction, naturally only of its sadder side, and of conflict between cotton sharecroppers on one hand and "first tenants" and landlords on the other. "It knocks thousands of fellows like me out of a crop. The ground is just laying there, growing up in weeds."

* * *

Sabir brought Hayat to me today. He says that she may be able to help me with her healing powers. I look at her and see her embroidered mouth, and want to tell her that she should go and practice her magic on someone else. She smiles at me. I wince at the sight of her blackened teeth and believe she is truly a witch. When she extends her hand to offer me something, I notice the markings on her arms and I know for sure that she is not like the rest of us here.

She holds some weeds and leaves in the palm of her hand. I look, I have nothing to say. A beetle moves between the dead leaves. She collects it into her cupped hands and shakes vigorously. Then she blows into the space between her thumbs and throws the leaves into the air.

The leaves drift down slowly and settle on different parts of me. The beetle lands upside down on my belly. Its legs struggle for a foothold. Sabir picks the insect up and flings it into a corner. I shut my eyes to tell them I don't want any more of this circus they've put on for me, or perhaps for their own entertainment.

This crazed woman from Kurile, did she know how far she was coming from home when she got onto that ship with Haji the Healing Man?

"God only knows why we left Texas, 'cept he's in a moving mood," said a woman whose agony at tearing up roots creased her face with deep lines.

Many families comforted themselves with the thought of returning home when the drought and Depression were over.

A pregnant Oklahoma mother living without shelter in Imperial

Valley while the men bunched carrots for money to enable them to move on asked my father for directions. "Where is Tranquility, California?"

Bulbul came to me today and told me that I should let Hayat heal me—he says that the cut she made on Anarguli's neck has helped to heal the wound, that it has given her back the words she had forgotten to use. He does not mention whether she can use her eyes again, and I don't want to tell him that it is probably the winter air that has dried the wound on her head, and the shock of the incision on her neck that gave her back the words.

He doesn't notice that Anarguli cannot see at night. And he has not spoken of the swelling where her baby grows even as the food she eats shrivels like a longing passed over and forgotten.

Bulbul takes me out into the courtyard again. It is snowing. I see the dog digging a hole in the ground, looking for food, perhaps. I worry that he may begin to dig up the graves along the edges of the courtyard. He has not eaten for days, except for the scraps Sabir saves for him.

I see the camel now, and the mule. Both are haggard and obviously hungry. The camel's eyes are glazed over with sleep or just the fatigue of waiting. And the mule, he would be better off dead.

I see the dog sniffing at the air around the mule.

The ground is white with snow, and in the distance I can see the gray blanket which will descend upon us like a plague.

* * *

With bedding drenched by rain while he slept in the open, with a topless car and a flat tire, an Oklahoman with the usual numerous dependents said to my father, "Pretty hard on us now. Sun'll come out pretty soon and we'll be all right."

I awoke this morning with the sense that something was going to change here, that these past several days of nothingness were just a prelude to a disaster.

Maybe it's just the fact that I really haven't been here since the fever took me away. And now that I'm back I expect something to go wrong, not that anything has gone right even in my dreams.

The pinched-face man is called Gulabuddin Shirazi. Waris and the others refer to him as Gul Agha, which roughly translates to Mister Rose. I want to laugh every time I see his miserable face and then think of his grand name, better suited to a comic book character.

Gul Agha has never really liked me. I can tell from the way he glares at me, with narrow eyes and a snarl on his thin lips. Last night when Qasim brought me my bowl of gruel (I don't move around much; my legs feel like sponge when I try to get up), Gul Agha spat in my direction and then very deliberately wiped his mouth with a grimy sleeve, his gaze trained on me the whole time. Waris told him to wipe the spit from the floor. Mister Rose fumed at him with hatred glowing in those narrow slit-eyes. He refused to do what Waris asked and instead spat again, staring at me long and hard. When Sabir got up and asked him why he was spitting on the floor and not into his tin can, Mister Rose said something softly, the words hissing ominously through his clenched teeth: *It is my country; I can spit where I want and you cannot stop me.*

Then he clutched at his breast pocket, where I believe he keeps his red book, and shouted words at Sabir, looking at me as he finished his recitation:

Note well the effect
Of a destitute orphan's sigh:
A hundred celestial battlements collapse.

Sabir did not speak. Instead he reached into the hearth for a handful of ashes which he threw over the globs of bloody phlegm. He turned to me and mumbled something to Waris. Both men walked out of the kitchen and I knew that something was being said about me, this Firangi who had no business in this country, in this asylum, in this wretched kitchen, eating into meager supplies and taking up space on the floor of the only warm place in this frozen wasteland.

It was quiet for a moment, then suddenly there was the sound of howling from the far corner of the kitchen, like a dog barking at the moon. I rose up on my elbows and saw Gul Agha screaming and gesticulating like a wild man. He was crawling on all fours toward me. In his hand he held the tin can full of phlegm. I could see that he wanted to throw the spit at me and I held up my quilt like a shield, my only defence against the assault I knew was coming. Bulbul rushed forward and threw himself on Gul Agha, pinning him to the floor. Noor Jehan ran out, calling for Waris. I could hear Anarguli whimpering behind the curtain and Qasim had begun to sob. Mister Rose was still screaming when Waris and Sabir hurried back into the kitchen. He kept repeating the word Qatil, Killer, over and over again. And he kept his gaze fixed on me, loathing in his eyes and in the twitching of his mouth.

Waris and Bulbul carried Gul Agha out of the kitchen. I had no idea where they were taking him—it had snowed heavily during the day and the only other place with a roof was my cell where the drums of water had been stored. I didn't really care where they took him as long as he was taken someplace where I didn't have to see him, and where he could not look at me the way he does, with so much hatred.

When Bulbul came back he told me that Gul Agha had been put in the shed with the animals. It was warmer in there than in the cell, and there was still some dry grass on the floor which would shelter him from the cold. I was wishing he would freeze to death when Bulbul began to tell me Gul Agha's story. About how he had taken his family from their village in the north after the drought killed his animals and crops, and even his youngest child who was born like a small animal with eyes that could not see and a mouth that did not cry.

Gul Agha had seven children, and after years of the war, after many of the villages had been abandoned or destroyed, he decided to head south toward the city where he had heard that food was being handed out to refugees like him. He and another family hired a tractor and loaded whatever they could carry from their homes into the trailer. They traveled for many days over the high mountain passes—the snow made it impossible for the tractor to cross much of the terrain, and the trailer would often get stuck in the deep ruts and craters blown into the land by bombs. Gul Agha and the other men, some only young boys, decided that they must walk and lead the tractor over this narrow trail, letting the women and girls stay in the trailer.

After many days their caravan made it through the pass into the valley, and it was at that point that the fire fell from the sky. Gul Agha says there were many planes and many bombs which fell around them like huge hailstones. The tractor was destroyed. The trailer, too, was hit. Gul Agha's wife and three of his children were killed, one was maimed, and two others died at the camp from hunger and cold. He was never able to understand why their small caravan was attacked, and he has never forgiven himself for letting his family remain in the tractor while he stood by as the bombs fell and annihilated everything he had ever loved.

When Gul Agha reached the refugee camp he was told that U.S. warplanes had attacked a party of rebels, killing eleven of them but missing the tall man who appeared to be the leader of the party and who walked beside the trailer, guiding it over the rough ground.

Gul Agha is not a tall man, Firangi, you can see that. But that day he was carrying his young son on his shoulders and had covered him with his chaddar to keep him warm. That child is still in the camp, perhaps, although many children froze to death that winter, and with no one to care for him now he is probably dead too.

I cannot sleep. I keep hearing the dog barking and the mule braying and the camel grunting in this still night hushed with snow. I look out at the snow-covered courtyard and see the footprints of a man burned into the white shell. I see a man carrying a child on his shoulders because the child has no legs. The child holds onto his father with hands that have been burned by the sun and are dark, the skin cracked and bleeding.

The snow is thick; it covers the many wounds on the earth and it conceals the sorrow which runs beneath it.

No one has attacked the asylum. Perhaps the war is over.

Waris says that when the snow covers the ground it is not easy for the rebels to move through the mountains. He knows that some of them in the north use young boys to carry provisions through the narrow passes. The children live on weeds and roots, and carry guns and ammunition on their thin backs because of the promise of food once they reach the rebel camp. The rebels need the children because they are small enough to squeeze into the tight passages carved out by the wind and water when it flows in abundance into the lavender valleys below.

Sabir says it has been quiet because it's not easy for warplanes to find targets in this weather. I want to tell Sabir about global positioning satellites and laser-guided systems which demolish buildings and kill people with the push of a button, without seeing them, without knowing them. Perhaps it is better not to speak and to let all of them rest. It has been so tiring, living in fear, waiting for the end.

Last night the dog attacked the mule, killing it and then eating the flesh that hung from its bones. Sabir wants to shoot the dog, but there is nothing to shoot it with. Waris wants to let the dog go, to leave the compound. He is clearly distraught, arguing with Sabir about granting the dog mercy. Sabir refuses to come in when evening falls, and Waris worries about him.

Bulbul says that the dog was hungry, that's all. He is not a mad dog, just driven mad with hunger.

When I saw the snow outside the shed stained with blood, I wanted to vomit. There was offal all over the place, long strips of gut spilling out of the mule's belly.

Its eyes were not completely shut, and its mouth hung open, a blue limp tongue, its end stuck to the snow that must have melted from the heat of its dying breath, and then frozen again when the breath vaporized into mist and obliterated the memory of the night before.

eight

The silence of this place is boring a hole in my heart. I have begun to read my words to myself just so there is something here other than the wind and the dance of the dust, and the long pauses between thought and speech which carry many meanings that I have not yet learned to understand.

Even when they argue they wait until a thought has been born and nurtured on parched tongues. Only when it is well-rounded does that thought dress itself in words, only when the hard edges of need and hunger and desperation have been chiseled into some semblance of acceptability does it find the arrow on which it travels toward its adversary.

I do not know if that is the way these people talk among themselves ordinarily, waiting for the words to be measured on their tongues before being expelled into the still air. Sometimes I think it is hunger that stretches the silence and strings it across the sky above this courtyard, like a tent or veil covering the secrets of women, hidden from sight, living in silences deeper than the graves we have dug recently for two of the men from the basement, and for the murdered mule.

Noor Jehan has not spoken much for several days now. She nursed me back to health, or back from the dead, and does not come to this corner at all, as if I must be avoided now that I am whole again, now that I can see her again as a woman.

She does not talk much to Waris either; I often see her going behind the curtain separating Anarguli and Hayat from us. Whenever she emerges I hear her sighing, and at night I can hear her whispering to Waris or humming a lullaby to Qasim. The boy has become a skeleton and his face is pale and miserable, a constant cold plaguing him. Noor Jehan tries to keep him clean but it is a losing battle—he has cold sores around his mouth which he licks to keep them from cracking in the dry air. His eyes are hollow now, and I try to read the words trapped inside them, but all I can see is his misery and the hunger which must consume his gut as it does mine.

We are sustaining ourselves on tea and the crusts of dried naan that Noor Jehan would feed to the mule. The tea itself is pale and weak, tasteless. Obviously we have run out of sugar, and the lumps of molasses that Sabir brought from the village have disappeared, leaving only a trace of golden flecks at the bottom of the saddle bag which was once strapped around the mule.

Bulbul says we should have eaten the mule after the dog killed him. Waris has a dark cloud cross his eyes when he hears Bulbul talking like this, making light of the delicious mule pilaf we could have had. *Khar pulao*, he says, and laughs. Sabir joins him, telling Waris that God would forgive us for eating the flesh of a cloven-hoofed animal because these are the circumstances in which we have found ourselves, and if God is Rahim and Rahman, Merciful and Beneficent, then khar pulao would be acceptable even to the staunchest believer.

Waris does not share their laughter. His face is dark now. The thought perches itself on the edge of his tongue but does not leave the stillness of his mouth.

I have begun to walk around in the snow now, after Bulbul outfitted me with a pair of boots he says he found in the rubble of the collapsed barracks. It seems Bulbul has a cache of goods which he finds and hoards and brings out when the time is right, bribing me with something I desperately need, reminding me of the treasures that will be his once we are out of here.

I think of the orange parka and the yellow corduroys and I want to weep. These have no laces, but that is the least of the problems. One of them has a mouth which has fallen open, and the other has a hole in the bottom. Bulbul has fashioned some kind of fastening for me from the dried and twisted mule gut he salvaged from the heap where Waris and Sabir buried the remains of that animal. The parts that could feed the dog have been buried in a drum and covered with snow. At least the dog will eat well. And at least I can get out of the kitchen and feel the soft layer of snow covering the courtyard like a white gauze bandage.

I stood for what seemed like hours at the edge of the compound near the wall, and tried to make out the place we repaired with bricks made from hard earth and effluence. There seems to be no trace now of the gaping hole through which I entered this world. All the fissures around the edges of the hole have been plastered over with rivulets of mud, and there are so many graves now that I cannot even remember which wall it was that spelled my fate with the brittle points of jagged teeth. There are small graves where the children are buried, larger ones that hold the bodies of nameless men, and an unmarked pit where the head and carcass of the mule were interred as if it, too, had been part of this war.

We have not eaten a meal, or what was passed off as a meal, for several days now. Karim Kuchak has been shouting from the basement; I have heard him hurling abuse at Waris and Sabir, calling them greedy thieves and one-legged, one-eyed bandits. Bulbul tried to explain to him that there is no food for anyone, that all of us are hungry, but he just snarled at him and smirked while calling him khazolak, an effeminate man, a man who has lost his honor and become like a woman.

Tell that guday, that lame man, to run off to the nearest village and fetch us some food, tell that mangak, that rat-faced woman, to stop eating it all up, tell that ruund, that one-eyed man, to stop hoarding the food and let us eat.

Karim Kuchak shouted this and we all listened in silence, as if there were no words left with which to defend our collective honor. And to think that all this invective was coming from a small, deformed creature who had crowned himself king of the trash heap, lord and master of the unwanted.

Bulbul laughed while telling me Karim Kuchak's story. Later at night, when Waris and Sabir and Noor Jehan had fallen asleep, he spoke to me about the time when he had known hunger after his mother disappeared, taking Gulmina and a few coins in change with her.

I was bringing in very little at the time, you see. Not many would part with a few coins because there was not much money to go around, even to buy bread for a family that would earlier have eaten lamb and chicken regularly. Everybody was hungry and my sister was hungrier than all of us, not able to eat, or not able to keep down whatever she ate. My mother asked my Uncle Sangeen to go find medicine for Gulmina but he refused, saying there wasn't enough money to buy bread, so how was he supposed to buy medicine?

My mother wept and pleaded with him, but he would just beat her or show her the back of his hand, threatening to strike her if she spoke about Gulmina's illness again. Gulmina was nothing but a heap of bones—she had beautiful eyes, my sister. Brown eyes that changed color with the time of day. At some point all that was left of her were her eyes, but they had no light in them, my friend. They were like holes filled with darkness.

One evening, after I came home with some pieces of bread from the tandoor where I worked, my mother asked Sangeen Kaka once more about medicine for Gulmina. My sister had just taken a bite from a scrap of naan I brought for her, and my mother was trying to spoon some hot tea into her mouth. We watched as Gulmina threw up the liquid and pieces of naan, her pale face shadowed over with distress and exhaustion. My mother held her, trying to ease the retching, and I watched in silence as her belly heaved and brought up the air which filled it and all the empty spaces in her thin body. She was still hunched over the floor when my uncle stepped forward and slapped her, saying that she had wasted precious food and wasn't worth the effort of keeping her alive. My mother threw herself over Gulmina, trying to protect her. My uncle kicked my mother's back; she fell forward, burying Gulmina beneath her. I was too frightened to move, but I remember worrying that Gulmina would not be able to breathe with her face in the vomit. And I remember my mother's tears when she raised herself to face me.

That night, while Sangeen Kaka slept, she woke me up and asked me for the few coins I carried in my pocket. She said she needed the money to buy medicine, to take Gulmina to a doctor or a hakeem who could heal her with herbs and would not ask for much money. I gave her what I had and watched as she covered herself and my sister in the great shawl she had worn ever since I could remember. It was a red shawl, faded now to a dirty brown and torn in many places, but it would keep her warm in winter and shield her from the sun in summer, and protect her from the eyes of hungry men.

Sangeen Kaka took me across the border shortly afterward. We traveled part of the way on the back of a truck bringing food supplies from a neighboring country. Sangeen Kaka knew the driver who had promised to help him look for a job once we got across. But when we reached the border he asked us to get off the truck and take the route across the mountains. We had no papers and the police at the border would not let us through without them. We walked across the mountains for several days. My feet were bleeding by the time we got to the city. I wanted to cry but was afraid of my uncle's anger, afraid of being called a woman. When we reached the city we made our way along a sewage drain that ran for miles and miles beside a camp where there were many others like us, come from across the border. I had to take off the shoes I was wearing because my blisters had burst and the skin was sticking to the plastic sole. At a tea stall where my uncle stopped to ask about a friend who had lived in this camp for a while, I removed the shoes but I was ashamed to let the men at the stall see my mangled feet. When one of them asked what had happened to make them look like raw meat, my uncle laughed and told them that I was lucky to have feet at all, whatever shape they were in, for I was the son of a man with no legs and a woman with no honor.

We have been waiting for something to happen, something to deliver us from this awful emptiness. Some days I want calamity to strike the compound, to put us out of our misery, to liberate us from this state of being and not being. I want to be found, even if it is too late. I want to know that this is not endless, this anguish of not knowing, of not having any dreams within which I can lose myself, finding what I have lost and what I may never find again.

Before I left home I learned of the mission Carlos was on at the time his plane was brought down. He was carrying two children with him who had been injured in a mine explosion. They had found the yellow care packages which our pilots dropped from the sky, and had run to their village with the packets of food meant to sustain them in the time of such great hunger. The village had been bombed sometime earlier with CBU-87s. Many of the bomblets had just lain in the fields, unexploded, waiting for something to touch them, to set them off. The children saw these yellow bombs, the size of soda cans, and rushed to pick them up. Their hands were blown up, arms torn off and flung across the fields. The girl lost part of her face; her brother had a hole in his stomach when they were brought to the base hospital in a wheelbarrow. Carlos was carrying them from the base along with several of our men who had been injured. They were headed to a place where they could be treated, but that was not to be. The plane was downed, and we never found out if it had been hit by a missile or if it crashed into the side of the mountain on a day when the clouds covered the earth with their infinite purity.

Noor Kaka is dying. I can tell by the look in his eyes— they are glazed over like the mule's eyes, and his breath comes in short spurts. I do not want to look at him but I don't know where else to look, and something compels me to watch this death, as if by doing so I will unravel the mystery of life itself.

Waris and Sabir attend to Noor Kaka as if he is their father, or father's father, and Bulbul works hard at keeping his grief hidden behind the grimace he pretends is from the pain in his feet. He says his feet hurt him in the cold—it may be the horribly twisted bones that stretch and push against his flesh in the dry air of winter. But I know that he grieves for Noor Kaka whose life was lived well, and whose death will mean the beginning of the end for all of us.

Sabir tells me that Noor Kaka spent many years as the keeper of the king's summer palace. He had a special ability with animals and was appointed by the king to look after his aviary and the collection of exotic animals in the palace. After the king was deposed, many of the animals were killed, but Noor Kaka got a job in the city at the local zoo. That is where he was found when the war was well into its tenth year—in the lions' cage, alone, with the bones of the animals that had starved to death, holding a man's wallet in his hand, telling anyone who cared to listen that the animals were starving and so he had fed them the stuffed birds that decorated the zoo superintendent's office. There was a bloodied shirt in the corner which Noor Kaka believed belonged to a man who had been fed to the lions when nothing was left to appease their hunger.

Noor came to Tarasmun for the same reason that most of the able-bodied and sane had made their way up the steep hill to this abandoned asylum—to find a place to rest before their final journey. Sabir says that when Noor goes, after we bury him, we will begin to bury parts of ourselves until nothing is left here except the sound of the wind whipping up the dust that leaps and dances on the graves.

I have begun to hear sounds which no one else seems to notice. Sometimes I think it is hunger which is driving me insane, then I consider that all of us here are hungry and I am the only one listening to these voices that sing to me and mock me and call me names.

Noor Jehan is trying her best to revive Noor Kaka's failing health. I want to tell her that it is no use, that he is old and weak and it is time for him to go, but she will not listen even if I could find the words. She comes up with strange concoctions prepared out of nothing, intended to give strength to Noor's fragile body. I saw her this morning with a lump of molasses which I thought had been consumed. She was clubbing it with a rolling pin and adding the beaten sweetness to the tea she was boiling for Noor. Waris looked at her and smiled, asking her where she had hidden the molasses for so long. She did not answer, but nodded in the direction of the curtain where Anarguli and Hayat sleep.

Bulbul told me later that Noor Jehan had been saving the molasses for Anarguli, whose belly is swollen like a watermelon, ready to burst with its offering of ripe, sweet flesh.

I cannot stand it anymore. I know I will lose my mind if I do not get out of here very soon. Noor Kaka is hanging on to life and Karim Kuchak is screaming from the basement like a madman. I don't know where he gets his encrgy from   maybc hc is cating thc rats which have built their colonies in that dungeon. And if he isn't, maybe I should tell him that according to the Book, eating crea-tures with claws is quite acceptable if these are the cir-cumstances in which he finds himself.

Hayat says she can heal Noor Kaka. Waris and Sabir do not stop her from doing what she wants. I am sure they know that the old man will die in any case, whether she does her mumbo-jumbo black magic or not. Or perhaps they are too tired to stop her. And indifferent and hol-low with hunger.

Bulbul tells me that Anarguli's time is near. I have not seen her in many days and even when I did, I couldn't see the swelling Bulbul speaks of. Perhaps Qasim the mute tells him these things—he sleeps with his mother behind that curtain and may have seen Anarguli's swol-len belly.

Bulbul is anxious; he irritates me by pacing up and down. I tire of watching him and all I want to do is sleep and not wake up, listening to my gut eat itself in desperation.

There is a sound of crying. I don't know if it is in my dream or if I have heard it coming from the kitchen. Per-haps Noor Kaka has died and they are grieving for him. What a waste of energy that would be.

Hunger is like an empty house where voices bounce off the walls and become dust on the barren floor.

* * *

144 🌳 FERYAL ALI GAUHAR

There is the sound of crying again. It is a woman's voice, soft and choked with despair. I see Noor Jehan in the corner, tending to the old man. I see her dab her face with her shawl and I know she grieves for him, for herself, for all of us.

Sabir tells me she asked him if she could slaughter the partridge he had named Inzargul, the flower of a fig tree, so that she could make a soup for Noor Kaka. He thought the partridge was almost dead anyway, pining for a mate and for springtime. It was better to kill it and let Noor Kaka taste it before either of them died.

Bulbul has disappeared. He did not return to the kitchen last night. A wind had been howling the whole day, and when snow began to fall, obliterating vision and muffling sound, he walked out of the kitchen and didn't come back. Waris wanted to go after him but Sabir pulled him back and told him to leave the boy alone. Perhaps he needs to be on his own. In any case, how far can he go with the wall protecting us from all sides, keeping us in and the others out?

I could not sleep last night because of this terrible hollowness in my gut. I began to feel nauseous and light-headed and made my way outside after the others had fallen asleep, or fallen into a stupor. I stumbled into the courtyard and stood before the tree which is now naked, and which serves to remind us of another time when we sat beneath it and soaked in the sun's warmth. I cannot imagine that there was a better time here, but the tree suggests that there was, even if I don't remember it.

I walked in the snow for a while until my body began to hurt, and when I made my way to the shed where the dog and camel slept I realized I could not feel my feet anymore. I pulled off my boots and began to massage them vigorously when my eye caught a glimpse of Bulbul's red scarf. At first I thought I was imagining things; my mind feels like it has no shape, and sometimes I believe I see and hear things which are not there. But the red scarf moved and then I heard the sound of scraping and chewing, and I smelled the odor of Bulbul's sweat and I knew he was here, in the shed with the animals.

I crawled on my knees to the corner where I saw the red scarf trailing on the earthen floor. My feet had lost sensation, I could not stand, my head felt it had nothing inside except some unbeatable will to live. When I reached the back of the shed I saw him. He was sitting on his haunches and in his hand he held a large bone, bits of dark meat clinging to it. He did not look up when I called to him. He turned to me only after he had pulled off a bit of the flesh and chewed it, swallowing it quickly as if it would leap out of his mouth and leave him hungry again.

He did not speak to me, but I knew that hunger had driven him mad, like the dog with whom he shared the bones of the dead mule.

Bulbul has not returned to the kitchen. I managed to get back, dragging one foot after the other, terrified of losing my feet and unable to get the image of the bone in Bulbul's mouth out of my mind.

I spoke to Sabir about what I had seen and almost wept, breaking down in front of this man who has not yet succumbed to hunger or cold or hopelessness. He left the kitchen quietly, his crutch wedged beneath the curve of his arm like an intimate friend.

Sabir returned to the kitchen alone. He spoke with Waris, who accompanied him to the shed this time. I watched these men as they went about the task of bringing Bulbul back to the fold, Bulbul who had strayed, Bulbul who was the red robin singing of another time, perched on a stalk of corn in a field where the earth covered the bones of his father.

Bulbul did not return. I wanted to go with the men to try to bring him back, but the searing pain in my feet did not allow me to stand. Noor Jehan helped me get the boots off, and then she asked Hayat to come and have a look at my feet. I let her do this, and I let Hayat massage my feet until I began to sense the blood rushing back, bringing with it pain and the relief of regaining the feeling I had lost.

Noor Jehan and I made our way to the shed late at night, after Waris and Sabir had checked on Noor Kaka and found him to be breathing and still alive. The men are exhausted, and part of their tiredness comes from not speaking about the fear that grows in their hearts. I have these words to comfort me, even if my fingers are becoming numb and I do not have the energy to continue writing. But it is either that or losing the only semblance of reality I have, these pages, these marks I make on them with Dr. Elisha's pen.

Noor Jehan asked me to come with her, as if my friendship with Bulbul would convince him to return to the relative warmth of the kitchen. I couldn't tell her that even if my feet didn't hurt so much, I didn't have the strength to stumble through the snowstorm which continues even as I write. As if she knew what I wanted to say, she offered me a piece of the brown molasses she had hidden in a sack behind the curtain. I took it and savored its rich sweetness, the fullness of the fruit buried inside.

Bulbul was hunched over beside the camel in the shed. He lay on the bare floor, the dog alongside him. He did not open his eyes when we crouched near him and called his name. I feared he was dead, but I could see his nostrils moving, and tears caught in the web of his shut eyes. He was whispering to himself, or perhaps to us, letting the words shape the terrible torment he suffered, the unthinkable humiliation of having eaten the flesh of a mule. I tried to raise him to his feet but he pushed me away, and I did not try to touch him again. He was babbling by now, something about *sharam* and *ghairat*, shame and honor, and the spit on the edges of his mouth formed white circles of regret on his face.

Waris and Sabir and I had to lift Bulbul up to bring him back into the kitchen. He was practically frozen and delirious, having spent two days in the open. Perhaps it was the warmth of the animals that kept him alive. Or perhaps it was his will to survive even this humiliation. Or the dream that he would find himself in America one day.

I have given up that dream. I know I shall never leave this place, and even if I do, this place will not leave me, ever.

I woke in the middle of the night again, hearing the

sound of a woman's weeping. The kitchen is warmer now—Waris braved the storm last night and chopped a branch off the tree in the middle of the courtyard. Sabir said this was the only way to survive now, to keep ourselves warm. He wanted to bring the surviving inmates from the basement up into the kitchen, and Noor Jehan voiced her concern about Anarguli being among these madmen. Sabir said that Anarguli would be alright, that it was more important to save the lives of these men than to maintain her sense of seclusion.

We now have Karim Kuchak and four others with us, besides Noor Kaka, Gul Agha, the man with the square head and large ears who refuses to die, and the boy with the frostbitten feet.

There is no place to stretch one's legs while sleeping, so we sleep leaning against the walls. This is probably how we will be found, sitting up, waiting.

It is Noor Jehan who weeps every night. I thought it was Anarguli, terrified of what will happen when the time for her baby comes. But Anarguli seems to be unaware of what is going on around her, perhaps because she cannot see in this dark space. Hayat hovers around her all the time, stroking her hair, adding yet more things to her silver braid. And Qasim sits listlessly beside Anarguli, his wooden cart now forgotten and discarded in a corner. I remember that I had promised to fix its fourth wheel, but there seems to be no purpose now in fixing anything.

Bulbul has recovered but does not speak. He looks away from me every time I try to meet his eye. I can see the shame burning in his eyes, and I want to tell him that it's alright, that this is what one must do when one finds oneself in peculiar circumstances. And then I want to laugh, and cry, and run out of here as far as my fricking feet can carry me.

Waris and Sabir spent some time outside this morning. They took the axe with them, probably to chop more wood. They do not go near the bomb buried in the rubble—that is where several trees fell in that attack, but they steer clear of the devastated barracks, fearing the worst. Sometimes I feel I can hear the choked cries of a child buried beneath the rubble, or the labored breathing of an old man desperately trying to keep his lungs from collapsing on him, like the roof of the barracks has crushed his ribs but perhaps not his spirit.

Sometimes I think I see the ground moving beneath me, like it must have the day the news of her husband's death reached my sister. She told me later that it felt as if the world was spinning; she heard voices around her, the chaplain offering to say a prayer for the fallen man, faint scratchings in the dust of her home, her devastated life. She said she felt as if she was walking on a surface that kept her afloat, her feet not really touching the ground. She saw the chaplain and the officer to the door, her heart wooden and quiet, and it was after the door clicked shut behind them that she crumbled to the floor of her living room, beating the chintz-covered sofa with her hand, yelling at Carlos, angry with him for having left her and their child who would never know his father now. That was what my mother heard on the phone, as she waited for what she feared most all those days after Carlos was sent to fight for a way of life he had seen advertised in catalogs, the kind that devour Bulbul's imagination. Carlos had come across the southern border from Mexico, traveling in the desert on the back of a pickup truck, left to die with his mother and four others who, like them, had opted to negotiate the wilderness of the desert rather than waste away in the certainty of unending poverty.

Mama was baking brownies the day we heard that Carlos had died. The fragrance of dark chocolate burned against the sides of the steel pan lingered in the air of our home like the sorrow hanging over my sister's eyes. My mother repeated over and over that the child had been orphaned before it even entered the world.

I had just come back from the game of one-on-one I played with our neighbor, Gary. I won that game, shooting the last basket as a layup, sneaking past Gary while he tried to balance himself on his big, clumsy feet. I kept telling myself that if I worked hard enough I might just make it onto the varsity team. That would have been one way to pay for college; the other was to work nights. And then there was that other choice, to give up my dreams and join the army, fighting for my country, or at least convincing myself of that in order to find a meaning to another man's life and then his death.

I did not join Waris and Sabir because I really don't care if we have firewood or food or water to keep us alive. But I don't want them to cut down the tree in the middle of the courtyard. For some reason I feel as if that would be the point of no return, when we begin to cut away our limbs to feed the fire that consumes us.

Noor Kaka is slipping away. But even as the breath leaves him, he speaks of the things he has seen and remembers from many years ago. He does not address anyone in particular; perhaps he does not see anyone around him with his failing vision and his dying breath. He is hardly audible, but I can still hear him tell the story of how he gathered the peaches and pears and pomegranates ripened to perfection in the valleys of Kulghoo and Tootoo and Hisaruk. Thousands of camels carried this precious fruit to the darbar of the king in another country, many miles beyond the river and the black mountains. The caravan passed beside the royal garden with its tall cypress trees reaching a height of a hundred feet, holding each other by the hand and rivaling each other in beauty. The camels themselves were tall and proud creatures, the finest of their kind, bearing the treasures of their country on their sturdy, pyramid backs.

Noor Jehan encourages Noor Kaka to drink the tea she has made. I believe it is more of an effort to keep him quiet, to preserve the breath inside him. Noor Kaka looks at her and calls her his daughter, zma lur, and then he closes his eyes and sleeps.

I hear a terrible sound, a muted bellowing, the dying gasp of an animal. I know I am dreaming of terrible things and, much as I try to stay awake, my eyes are heavy and my heart is filled with lead.

What was that sound, sergeant? That gasp which came from behind the door when you kicked it open, sir? When you rushed into that room in the brick hovel on the edge of the neighborhood where we saw that girl with the dark eyes and the body of a temptress? What was that, sergeant? That shriek as you shut the door behind you and unzipped your pants and forced yourself on that girl with the dark eyes? What was that smell, sergeant, as you left quickly, discarding the bloodied shirt you wore when you put three bullets through her head, aiming between those dark eyes? Was that the stench of burning flesh, sir? Was that the stench of your soul burning in the Fire of Hell? Did you come back to base camp and wash yourself, sir? Did you manage to get the smell out from under your skin, from beneath

*the folds of your penis, the recesses of your nose, the thicket of your
hair, your pale blue eyes, sir?*

Karim Kuchak sleeps between the legs of the large-eared
man and another with a long head and an emaciated body.
He is calmer here and does not abuse us anymore. It's
amazing how easily these people are placated, with just a
little warmth or a spoonful of liquid passed off as tea.

Noor Jehan does not sleep, nor does Bulbul. Normally she retires behind the curtain at night but this
night she stayed with us in the kitchen, first tending to
Noor Kaka and now stroking Bulbul's hair. He has still
not spoken and Noor Jehan talks to him with the voice
of a mother, telling him that it's alright, that he is not a
lesser man for having eaten the flesh of a mule, that this
is what war drives respectable people to do. She speaks
to him of the time when she was still in the village and
saw grown men weep over the bodies of their dead children, blown to pieces by the bombs that fell on the field
where they played soccer. And she told him about the
garbage dumps where often she would see the limb of
a child torn at the joint and found among the rubble of
people's lives. She spoke calmly, as if she wanted Bulbul
to know that all of them had seen their share of suffering, that all of them had been driven mad at some point,
mad with grief and mad with the agony of loss.

I made my way in the dark toward her, stumbling
over limbs and Sabir Shah's crutch, and listened to her
story, which she spoke in words I had begun to understand, words which were part of the language of
absence.

* * *

Waris Khan and I are cousins. My father left the village many years ago when I was still a child, and traveled to a land beyond the seas. He would send us money and sometimes return with gifts of soft velvet blankets with images of cats, or perhaps tigers—I was too young to know the difference—and radios that played the sweetest music, the songs of Qamar Gul, speaking of her beloved's dark eyes and the gaping hole in her heart which was her beloved's absence.

I was one of several girls in the family. My sisters were beautiful and fetched a good bride price when they were married. But I seemed not to be worth much, and even though my father laughed and called me his little dark camel, I knew that I did not measure up among the other young women who had suitors paying large sums of money for their hands in marriage. It was my cousin Waris who finally asked for me, and much as my mother wanted to wait for a better proposal, my father insisted that the offer was a good one: there would be some cash, and the rest of my dower would be made up with the promise of a decent life as the daughter-in-law of the village muezzin, a respectable man with few means but great honor.

Waris Khan himself had learned to be a carpenter. When the war began and the mosque was hit during Friday prayers, killing his father and injuring so many others, Waris became a builder and repaired it within a few days so that there would be a place for men to worship Allah. The men in the village knew he had a gift, that his hands were able to create beauty out of the most ordinary materials, and they began to ask him to repair their damaged homes, erecting walls and constructing doors out of fallen trees. Waris did not ask them to pay him with money, knowing that there was not much to go around, but he gladly took whatever they could give him, sometimes a chicken, other times a dozen eggs, and once a newborn lamb whose mother had stepped on a landmine while grazing in the field.

We were happy, as much as anyone can be in times of hardship. When I became heavy with our first child, Waris embraced me so *tightly I thought I would lose consciousness. He said that we would name our son after his father, and that we would send him to school so that he could learn to read and write and be a good man in the future. Our son was born in the winter but he did not live to see spring, and I grieved for that lost child until summer turned our fields to gold and the sky became the color of lapis. When I told Waris that there was another child who would be coming to us at the time of the harvest, he said we must prepare carefully for his arrival.*

Waris loved children, but his own never lived for more than a few months after they came into this world. I became distraught each time I lost a child, and began to think of myself as worthless, the little dark camel my father would laugh at. There was a teacher in our village who had been to the city to study, like Sabir Shah, and he told Waris that our children would not live because they were born of the same blood, the two of us being cousins. Waris didn't believe him, but took his advice and left for the city where I would be seen by a doctor who would help us keep our next child.

We collected our few belongings and said goodbye to our families. My mother wept to see me go—she said she knew she would never see me again. I tried to reassure her but she just shook her head and told me that daughters do not belong to their mothers; when they marry they become the responsibility of their husbands until they die. Once a daughter leaves her home she becomes a stranger to her mother, and I was becoming that stranger now.

The journey to the city was difficult. I was carrying the child in my womb, and I stumbled often on the rough mountain paths leading out of the village. Waris was using our mule to carry our belongings. Along the way he took off the bundle of clothing and grain that the mule was carrying and asked me to sit on top. He carried our belongings and I rode the mule, and that is how we arrived in the city, expecting to find a doctor who would help me bear the child we wanted to nurture and love.

Waris knew a man at a hospital who guided him to a woman doctor who specialized in diseases of the womb. The next morning we made our way from the home of our friends near Puli Baghumoomee in the center of the city to the hospital in Karte Se. Waris made me sit on the back of the mule, seeing my exhausted state. We were traveling along the side of the street when the mule became frightened by the noise of trucks passing by. He bolted into the middle of the street, throwing me off first. I wasn't hurt much, and asked Waris to go after the mule which had been hit by the side of a truck. Waris ran into the middle of the street and tried to get the mule out from under the truck. I watched him as he struggled to free the animal's legs from under the wheels, and then I saw several men jump off from the truck and begin hitting Waris with the butts of their rifles. They kept accusing him of having caused the accident that damaged their truck. They said they would punish him like the others who had tried to obstruct their path, and they dragged him to the back of the truck. I rushed forward, shouting at them to leave Waris alone, to leave my husband alone. But it was already too late—they had thrown him into the back of the truck, and when they saw me they said that I had no business being out in the streets like a woman with no morals. The men got into the truck and began to drive away. I ran after the truck, pleading with them to let my husband go. I could hear the mule braying and the noise of the truck in the distance as it drove off, leaving me alone on that street. I had no idea what to do, and for a while I just sat in the middle of the road next to the injured mule, wanting to die, to end a life that had nothing in it now but misery.

Several men passing by stopped and asked me what had happened. I told them about Waris being taken away by the men in the truck, and they assured me that he would be back, that it was just a game these people played with the lives of those who have no power. I didn't want to leave that place where I had been separated from my husband, but the men said it wasn't safe for me to be on my own. I let them have the name of the family we were staying with, and they took me back, dragging the mule along on his injured legs.

Waris returned to me after many days. I had wanted to end my life, believing that I would never see him again. I had no one else I could turn to, and so I turned to Allah and asked Him to take my life and give it to one more deserving. But He is infinitely kind in His mercy, and He let me live. Although I had already lost the child in my womb, He let me live.

Waris was pale and haggard when he came back. He told us of his ordeal, of having jumped off the back of that truck once they left the city and were headed for some outpost in the mountains, where the commander of these men waited with the loot they were carrying in barrels loaded onto the truck. At first Waris thought the barrels contained food and other items stolen from people in the city. But when the lid of one of the barrels fell off on a particularly bad road, he peered into it and was horrified to see the body of a man with his hands and feet tied with a rope. He had been dead only a little while—his body was still warm, and there was spit on his mouth where he must have licked it when his soul escaped his body.

That is when Waris decided to jump. He said it was better to die trying to escape than to die like that man in the barrel. Waris injured his leg when he leaped from the truck, and took several days to get to the nearest town to ask for directions to the city. When he arrived at the house where I had waited for so many unending days, he just held me and then collapsed on the floor. I did not tell him that I had lost our third child. I did not want him to suffer more than he already had.

After a few days we got news from the village. We were told that disaster had struck the day after we left. A caravan of trucks stopped at the village and told the people to give them food and clothing and anything else of value. The men of our village resisted and were shot. The women, old and young alike, were taken away. The children had hidden from these men, but couldn't survive on their own for too long.

Waris wanted to go back immediately. I pleaded with him to let things be, saying it was probably too late, that he needed to rest and heal. But he wouldn't listen and said he would go on his own, that it was necessary for him to find out what had happened to his family.

We made our way back to the village without the mule, whose legs were now twisted and useless. When we got there we found nothing except the wind and dust and heaps of mud which used to be our homes. There was no one around. We were ready to turn back when we heard a baby's cry, weak but still carrying the sound of life. We rushed into a house whose walls were still intact. There were bodies of several children on the floor, huddled together as if they had been trying to keep each other warm. When we touched them, they were already stiff with cold. The baby, a tiny little thing with large eyes, was lying between the older children. He had survived, and even if he has lost his words he is the story I wanted to tell you, my son. He is Qasim, a gift from God, the child we did not have, the child for whom I live.

nine

We ate well today. Waris and Sabir were triumphant in their mission and carried back the dark, smelly flesh of that miserable camel who was worth little in life, but a lot more after he was ritually slaughtered, fulfilling the religious obligation of believers.

Sabir tells me it is the Festival of the Sacrifice, when the Prophet Abraham saw in his dream that he had made an offering of his young son to convince Allah of his faith. In the dream Allah switched Abraham's son with a goat. And in this dream of madness, we have replaced the goat with a dark-haired camel.

Today we had a delicious stew seasoned with Noor Jehan's special blend of spices—some rock salt and crushed black pepper. She even offered us dried pomegranate seeds after we ate, telling me they would help me digest the tough flesh of that ancient animal.

Everyone is happy. Karim Kuchak is laughing again, and the rat-faced man squeals with delight. Anarguli smiles too, and Hayat has a wide grin on her face which makes the tattoo around her mouth look even more like a mustache. Qasim has filled his belly to the extent that it now looks bloated and he complains of a stomachache. Noor Jehan rubs his belly and insists that Noor Kaka should eat only the soup, not the flesh, because it is not tender enough for his toothless mouth.

Noor Kaka laughs. There is a soft glow in the hearth this evening and a feeling that all will be well, despite the snow outside and the dread in our hearts.

When can I go home, sir?

She was in a diabetic coma when we found her, passed out in front of the television in her small unit in a gated community in the Fig Gardens. There was a cat sitting with her on the couch, staring at us with round, green eyes, meowing in a dolorous kind of way. The television was still on—I caught a glimpse of Jerry Springer and two large-breasted women lunging at each other for all it was worth.

Our lady of the condo was heavy too. It took everything out of me to lift her up with my partner and place her on the gurney before getting her into the ambulance. I checked her vitals—blood sugar low, heartbeat almost imperceptible. Her pupils were constricted, and her hands clammy and cold. When she opened her eyes, blue and pale, sunk in the flaccid flesh of her face, she did not speak. And when she finally did speak, I got the feeling that whatever she said was what I would hear for the many trips I would take as an emergency medical technician, fresh out of school.

I called ahead to the hospital to let them know what to expect, aware the whole time that there would be several others parked on gurneys along the hallway or laid out on beds, hooked up to monitors, peeing into bags and generally feeling alone despite the number of staff on duty in the emergency room. In all the time I spent taking people into the ER, most of them were old folks living alone or with a pet, or with others like them. Some were so old they couldn't remember their names, or perhaps that was not age, just the drop in their sugar level or blood pressure playing tricks with their minds. Or it could be that they hadn't heard their names in so long that they had forgotten them.

Some of them probably didn't have much to remember—the

lady of the condo who had been watching Jerry Springer before she passed out on her couch asked for her daughter. It was a neighbor who called 911, and the same neighbor who gave the hospital her daughter's phone number.

The daughter came. It was Friday night, she must have been out on the town—she wore a fake fur coat with large gold buttons. Her fingernails were long and curved, painted red and gold. She was heavy, like her mother, and she had the same pale blue eyes set in her ample face. She didn't want to stay long, and took off with her husband (his name was Elmo, he was bald and corpulent, like Elmer Fudd in the comic strip) as soon as the nurse told her they would keep the comatose woman for the night.

Call me, honey. Let me know when she comes round. Gotta go now, sweetie.

Bulbul has begun smiling again, although he doesn't talk much. He spends most of his time beside the curtain separating him from Anarguli and Hayat. Noor Jehan saves the strongest tea for him before she waters it down to stretch it for the rest of us. It's as if she has found another son in him, other than Qasim and the ones she lost.

Bulbul has something to smile about. The large-eared man, having heard of the night Bulbul ate the mule's flesh, has pronounced it quite alright to consume anything as long as one believes that Allah does not want us to suffer, that He always shows us a way, that it is up to us to find it.

His name is Haji Meer Abdul Hassan. Before the war, he had traveled far to complete his religious learning and performed the pilgrimage at Mecca many times, taking his mother with him on his last journey. Haji carried the old woman on his back throughout the pilgrimage, circling the Kaaba where pagan priests had placed idols for the people to worship, before the true faith was revealed and the idols smashed by the Prophet who declared that there was only one God and that was Allah. The old woman had not survived the grueling heat and the crowds, and was buried in the desert of that holy kingdom. Haji says it is an honor for a believer to die while paying the greatest homage to Allah. His mother died a fulfilled woman, and he returned to his village a satisfied man, a dutiful son.

It was only after his pilgrimage that things began to go wrong. On the evening of his return, his young daughter went missing. She was twelve, and Haji had hoped to marry her off in a year or two. He was asked to pay ransom for her but he refused, telling his family that his daughter would have no honor left once she came back. The little girl was found the next day, dead, on his doorstep.

I thought she was asleep, my little Zarsanga. She looked so peaceful, like my mother after we prepared her for the burial in Medina. Only when we carried her inside did I see the marks on her neck—she had been strangled, and her blood had turned black with shame at what they did to her while she was still alive. I could see that black blood beneath her fair skin, pale now, like corn before it ripens. I knew she must have struggled—there were cuts on her wrists where they tied her, and on her ankles too. She had not been visited by any man after she became a young woman, except her brothers and uncles. And now I knew that she had been touched, and violated, by men we had never seen or known.

Zarsanga had gone with the elder women in the family to collect water. After so many dry years, the journey to a mountain stream or a small spring took longer each time. She would leave early in the morning, carrying the water pot on her head—sometimes the women would not return till the afternoon, when food for the evening had to be prepared, the animals fed, the children washed, and the home cleaned. Zarsanga always looked forward to going with the women—she had been betrothed to my brother's son and she knew that in a year she would leave our home for that of her husband. It was as if she wanted to spend as much time as possible with her mother before the final separation.

I did not know then that this was how the parting would occur, with her death, with the shame and dishonor that her abduction brought us.

Haji did not complete his story. The other men had finished their meal and were listening to him, even Karim Kuchak who ordinarily never let anyone complete a sentence. I realized then that none of these people were insane—they had just found themselves in the middle of insanity and given up the fight to claim what was theirs.

Sabir told me later that Haji had left the village, never to return to his family. Sabir said that more than the shame of having had a daughter abducted and probably raped, Haji couldn't forgive himself for not trying to get her back. She was just a little girl, his girl, and in her eyes he had seen his own shame. Not the dishonor that was brought upon the family through no fault of hers, but of having been a coward when she needed him to stand by her, to love her the way a daughter should be loved.

* * *

I am having the dreams again, this despite the fact that my stomach is not aching with hunger and my head is not humming with fatigue. There was a time when I thought I would not survive this ordeal, but after the camel was slaughtered, after food was cooked once again and the fire was lit, I thought the dreams would leave me, that if I was to dream at all it would be of home and my mother and the life I left behind, to come to fight a war I no longer believe in.

In downtown Clovis there was an antiques store which sold old radios and Elvis records, and Coke bottles that looked like the bodies of curvy actresses wearing tight corsets in movies where men wore trench coats even when it wasn't raining. Most of the stuff wasn't really antique, not in the sense of being really old or even valuable. There were hair clips and teddy bears and baking tins and canisters of sugar. There were postcards and school report cards and baseball caps and Victorian camisoles and even a wooden toilet which must have sat in an outhouse, also wooden, also stained with the stink of human waste. A lot of this junk would be looked over and carefully guarded by old ladies in pink sweaters and blue hair, sometimes knitting booties for grandchildren, sometimes complaining about the arthritis that flared up on days when the fog rolled in across the San Joaquin Valley and shrouded everything in its mystery.

At the back of the store were plastic soldiers and war memorabilia locked in glass cabinets. I would stand for hours in front of the cabinet with the collection of gas masks and soldier uniforms from Vietnam. There were dog tags and wireless phones and playing cards, which must have kept the men and boys distracted from the boredom of the long pause between one killing and the next. I would wonder then who brought these things in, these bits and pieces of men's lives, these badges of courage or perhaps shame, or perhaps just plain old badges which must have shone when they were first worn across someone's chest.

In the dream I am looking into the cabinet. I see my reflection in the glass door. When I move away my reflection enters the cabinet and opens the door for me from within. I step inside. There is a searing stench of burning flesh. At the bottom there is a wireless phone with the sound of a crying child through the crackle and hiss of the static. I turn toward the door but it has swung shut and the handle has broken off like the limb of a dying tree. When I pick up the wireless set to call for help it crumbles in my hands, and the dust of its remains pours through the gaps in my fingers onto the glass floor of the cabinet. The sound is like rain falling on dry earth.

The snow has piled up outside the kitchen door and it is difficult to get out. Karim Kuchak and the others go down to the basement to relieve themselves. I can smell the stench all the way up here, and I know that I cannot go there, balancing above the excrement of a dozen others, piled up into putrefying mounds.

Anarguli is ready to burst now. I can see the bulge of her belly even beneath the dirty shawl she wears over her shirt. I try not to look at her, terrified that I will be dishonoring someone, her perhaps, her family definitely, even if her family does not exist or has forgotten all about her.

This business of honor intrigues me. It seems as if everything is connected to a woman's body—a man's honor lives inside the body of a woman, and when that honor is violated, it is a woman's body which must be punished.

I am learning these things now. I know my mother

would want to know about how the menfolk treat women
here, in this strange part of the world, and I can imagine
the look on her face when I tell her that they destroy the
women they love because they cannot bear to lose them
to another.

My mother was lost to another, but she always said
that leaving my father was the only way she could have
survived. There was only so much of his rage that she
could take, and only so many of the beatings which
came at midnight once the last bottle of beer had been
smashed against a piece of furniture or on the floor of
our home in Tranquility, California.

I remember the blood on her arms which had turned
black with shame. But that was not the same as the
shame which drove Haji Meer insane. Her shame lived
in her white body and chided her for having married a
man who had nothing to his name, not even the land
that held the bones of his ancestors. My father had nothing but his rage; even his name was not his own, and the
woman he had tried to make a life with was lost to another because he had no life to offer her, no words with
which to heal the wounds he inflicted on her.

*I am in the emergency room again. There is a young boy we have
brought in, unconscious, a stab wound in his rib cage pulsing with
blood. He is only fourteen. On the band of his neck there is a tattoo which identifies him as a member of a Tulane County gang. We
found him lying off Divisadero Street on the pavement, his blood
soaking the concrete. His pals called 911 and told us where to find
him. He comes to now and then, and mumbles something we cannot
understand.*

He is really young. His breath smells of alcohol. In the ambu-

lance we checked the level in his blood—it was four times higher than the acceptable limit. He has wet his pants, and there is vomit down the front of his T-shirt. On his face I can see the faint trace of a dark mustache. When he wakes up he asks for his mother. He speaks in Spanish, and I respond to him with a crude joke about big men who drink not needing their mothers when they want to pee. He grimaces, and I realize that each time he wakes up he feels the pain of the stab wound, and I want him to sleep again, not to wake while the odor of urine and vomit stick to his skin like a crest of disgrace.

In the emergency room there are more jokes and more pain as the nurse inserts the catheter into his penis. C'mon, son, be a man— Lord knows you're hung like one.

He needs to be given an enema, to flush his bowels. The nurse rolls him over on his side and I can see the blood spurting out from beneath the bandage—there are no stitches yet until the wound is cleaned. One of the nurses throws up the sheet covering him and pulls down his pants. The other one tells him to relax his buttocks, warning him that if he tenses up, the pipe in his rectum will hurt. The boy is screaming now: Stop, please, stop! Jesus Lord, help me, ayuda me, ayuda me, Mamá.

I look up at the woman who has just been wheeled into the space in hall one. She is young; her skin is pale and her hair dark. She lies on her back with her eyes closed. I can see traces of tears rolling down the side of her face. I am drawn to her as if she is someone I have known. I leave the young boy squirming with pain in the room and walk out into the hall toward her. I stand close and look at her face. It is Anarguli, and when she opens her eyes I see only dark tunnels that lead nowhere.

Bulbul is worried sick now. He believes that unless we seek help for Anarguli she will die in the process of giving birth. I try to tell him that he is worrying only because his stomach is full. When he was hungry, all he did was look for food, scavenging in the pits outside.

I regret having said this the minute the words leave my mouth. Bulbul does not respond to me. He just gets up and walks away. It is good that the snow outside the door has been cleared. At least he has a way of escaping his suffering and I have the space to deal with my remorse alone.

Noor Kaka is in good spirits. It is as if this old man has many lives, surviving one bad thing after another. He smiles his toothless smile at anyone, any time, for any reason, and Sabir reminds me that the Sufi poets say that in disaster or in the absence of disaster, one must remain the same. He tells me that the Wali, the leader, in his normal conscious state, tries in all sincerity to acquit himself of all his obligations to God.

Further, in whatever state he may be, he treats the people with unfailing kindness and affection. He spreads his graciousness on all creatures; and he bears with good cheer their malevolence. And without their requesting it, he prays to Allah to take good care of them and tries his very best for their salvation. He never takes vengeance on others, and he does his best to keep his heart free from malice against them. With all this he never tries to extend his hands on what belongs to others, and he does everything to keep away from greed. He keeps his tongue under control so that it does not speak ill of them. And he keeps his soul from seeing the failings of others, and he never fights with anyone either in this world or the other. He remains constant, true to his Maker, the Almighty, the Omnipresent Allah.

Noor has remained constant. All of them have remained

the same. Only I seem to have changed, and I don't know if that is a good thing or the only thing I can do in order to survive.

There is much one can do to survive. The extent of a human being's imagination when pushed against the wall is overwhelming. I think of Bulbul and the bone, and I think of the story Noor Kaka told us the day we ate the camel stew. He smacked his lips and sucked his fingers and then he told us about who he was, what he did for a living, and why he found himself here, among all the others who have nowhere else to go.

My sons, Waris Khan, Sabir Shah, Bulbul Jan, and you, Firangi Amreeki, I wish to thank you all for your kindness during the time of my illness. I know I was near death's door and I could see the Angel Israel beckoning to me, but Allah had other plans. Much as I wanted to pass out of this world and into the next, to stand before my Maker and beg forgiveness for any act of mine which caused suffering to another, seeking punishment or reward as Allah saw fit, I knew that there were certain things that had to be done before I passed over.

One of these things, my sons, was to tell you who I am. The other was to tell you that sometimes Allah rewards the ones He loves with riches in Janat ul Firdaus, and sometimes He presents these riches to His chosen ones while they are still on this earth. I had the good fortune of finding those riches while I lived, even if I have nothing now except the name of my Maker on my lips and devotion to Him in my heart.

You must think, here's an old fool, this man with torn clothes and hands worn down with hard labor and age. What riches could he have had, and if he did, where is that fortune now? you will be asking yourselves, my sons. I have thought many times of the words with which to describe this fortune to you, and then I have been afraid that you will think me a worse fool for having told you. But today I feel I must share this treasure with you, even if I have nothing to show that will make you believe my story.

My sons, I was very young when the king of our beloved country asked for a man to work in the grounds of his summer palace outside the city, in the shadow of the Hindu Kush. My father had been a gardener in the palace grounds and he told me there was a job for me to do. I was excited, for my father did not speak to me often—he spoke rarely at home, and even less to his children. So when he said he would like to take me to the summer palace to meet the keeper of the grounds and see if I had the necessary skills for the new job, I thought my heart would burst with joy. Not only was my father talking to me, he was going to show me the summer palace which none in the family had ever hoped to see.

I couldn't sleep that night. I asked my mother to wash my good shirt and I sat up polishing my shoes with the soot of the coal fire. I couldn't even eat the breakfast of naan and Suleimani chai my mother made for us. When we left the house, I looked at my mother and asked her to pray for me. She embraced me and whispered a prayer for me, then kissed my eyes. I waved goodbye to my sisters and younger brothers and walked rapidly to catch up with my father who took long strides and hurried through the alley, his gaze fixed on the ground. The food my mother had prepared for the journey was bundled into a scarf that he carried in one hand.

My sons, the journey to the summer palace was a long one, but perhaps not long enough for one who is young and full of longing to see the world. We were headed toward the Karez e Meer, outside the city. In front of us we could see the Hindu Kush glistening with fresh snow. The road leading to the foothills was shaded by ancient walnut trees, and often we would see caravans of Bactrian camels carrying fruit between their humps, their heads held high like boats afloat on the river.

The hills circling the city were covered with vineyards and orchards. Sweet, succulent raisins from the grapevines had been picked and laid out on the ground—I remember the scent of the fruit and the purple haze covering the hillside. There were many trees in this valley—pine and almond, mulberry and peach. And everywhere there was the fragrance of wild grass and lavender, making my head light and my heart even lighter.

There were brooks and springs everywhere. We could hear their music even before we came across them, quenching our thirst with the sweet, clear water. Above these water channels were the yellow leaves of autumn which played their own music before winter extinguished the life they held in their veins.

The town of Istalif lay before us like a pyramid, terraces with houses and fields leading to the pinnacle which was crowned by the shrine of a Sufi saint. Beyond Istalif we had to travel through a mountain pass that would close in less than ten days, opening again in the springtime when the snow melted and caravans passed through the Hindu Kush again. The ascent to this pass was gradual, but at a certain point the track suddenly became steep, causing our horses to slip on the frozen ground. We had to dismount and proceed on foot. One horse fell and plunged to his death. I did not dare look down into the ravine where he would have lain, the breath slowly slipping out of him.

The summit of the Hindu Kush is made of black rock, my sons, granite, hard and relentless. Against that black rock, the snow was of the purest white, and the sun would reflect on it and blind us, leading us toward the edge of the mountain, leading us to the many graves of those who had tried to pass through here before but who never made it to Kohistan, where we were headed.

To get to Kohistan you have to cross many rivers and water channels. Of the rivers you would know the Panjsheer, but you would not have known that if a man stood on its banks and held out his hands, *he would most certainly catch the fish that leap out of its cold froth-ing waters and offer themselves as a meal to a hungry traveler.*

My father did not stop for long, just long enough to feed him and me, or to catch some sleep under a poplar tree. We drank from the rivers or the aqueducts that the people of the villages had constructed in order to take the water to their fields. At a certain place my father told me to drink long and hard, for we were about to enter the valley of shifting sand, the Reg Ruwan, where the earth is soft and the sky far, and water just a thread in a madman's dream.

My father told me that Babar Badshah, the king of all kings, em-peror of all he surveyed, had described the Reg Ruwan as a stretch of sandy ground leading from the top of a hill to the bottom. Babar Badshah described the sound of drums that would erupt from the depths of that sandy track, and I wondered whether I too would hear the music of the desert.

It was sunset when we began to attempt the crossing of this stretch of moving sand. We walked toward the junction of two hills where the track began, and as soon as we stepped onto the sand, we heard the hollow sound of drums beating below the surface of the earth. My father told me it was a miracle we had heard the sound, for the drums are only beaten on Friday, the holiest of days, but perhaps it was the saint of Reg Ruwan who ordered the drumming for my ben-efit. My father smiled at me while telling me this, and my heart filled with pride at being this magnificent man's son.

My father told me that the sand had been carried to this part by the northern wind, the Bad e Purwan, which would blow with such force that souls traveling toward the heavens often lost their way and buried themselves in the sand until the wind passed, shifting the sand and covering the tracks of their journey.

After we crossed the Reg Ruwan, I turned back to look at the set-ting sun and saw the stretch of sand that cut through two mountains like a river, moving and pulsing toward the lavender fields of that magical place. I wanted the journey to continue for many years so that my father could tell me these stories, so that I could see the wonders that Allah had created for us to behold and to enjoy, but we were nearing our destination and all journeys have to come to an end, my sons, like mine will soon.

Noor Kaka stopped suddenly. None of us had dared to open our mouths while he spoke, and I had to keep Bulbul from interrupting the old man with a succession of questions he kept whispering in my ear: *What is this treasure the old man speaks of? Where is it? Where has he hidden it? Why does he take so long to tell us? Ya Khuda, I pray he doesn't die before he tells us about this treasure . . .*

But Noor Kaka stopped just before he got to the destination which had changed his life and made him a richer man. He stopped, took off his glasses, spat on them, wiped them on the edge of his filthy cuff, and placed them in his pocket. Then he smiled at us and said it was late, that he was an old man, that he needed his rest now, and that he would finish the story in the morning.

Anarguli has had the most beautiful baby one could imagine. The little girl came at around sunrise after several hours of labor, during which the men in the kitchen had to be sent to the shed to wait out the night. Noor Jehan and Waris asked me to remain in case there was a problem with the delivery. And Hayat refused to leave Anarguli's side, chanting strange incantations in her own language the whole night long.

Bulbul was sick with worry and did not even stay in the shed all those hours. Sabir told me he had vanished again and came back only when the sun began to appear from behind the mountains. That was about the time the little girl was born. Noor Kaka has named her Sahar Gul, the Rose of Sunrise.

Noor Jehan has sweetened our tea with the last of the molasses she was hiding in her secret sack. This is to celebrate the safe arrival of the newest member of our tribe. Sabir says that the birth of a daughter is not usually celebrated in these parts, but this little girl is the future, and if she lives, all our dreams will live on.

Bulbul beams every time he looks at Anarguli, who sits with the baby in front of the fire. Waris and Sabir have chopped up the desk and the broken chairs in the demolished office so we have some more warmth now. The baby is tiny, almost too small to live through the winter. When Noor Jehan asked me to cut the umbilical cord with the kitchen knife (I insisted we boil some water and clean it first), I feared that I would be cutting off the baby's only source of nourishment, for Anarguli did not seem to have the strength to feed her child, weakened as she was by hunger and disease.

But things in this miserable place do not happen as one expects them to. Anarguli appears to have regained her health and her vision, for she fixes her gaze on this child and does not see anything else. Noor Jehan has taken her behind the curtain several times to coax her to let the baby suckle her breast. I don't know if there is any milk for the baby in Anarguli's breasts. All I see is that the child is content and sleeps peacefully, while the men snore deeply, dreaming of Noor Kaka's hidden treasure.

Only Bulbul does not sleep, despite the relative peace

of the night. He comes to me often and wants to speak to me, but I am exhausted from my vigil during the birth, and all I want to do is sleep.

I shut my eyes and watch the baby's birth being played out against the inside of my eyelids. I watch my hands tremble as I cut its cord and clear its airways and listen for its breath and the cry which will announce its arrival. I close my eyes tighter, trying desperately to clear my head of everything. I still see things—I hear Hayat's chanting, Anarguli's moaning, and I see Noor Jehan take the umbilical chord and bury it in a corner of the room.

And what about my sister's baby? What has she named it? It was to be a girl and Carlos had wanted to name her after his mother, Maria, who perished in the desert along the border. Actually, she had lived to make it to the back of the sheriff's truck, and died on the highway when the truck was tail-ended by a young man talking into his cell phone and not watching the road. It was a Sunday, summer in California, with surfers returning from the beach, the sun clinging to them like the sand they carried in the pockets of their shorts. Maria was in the back of the truck when they were hit. Carlos always said that it was not the impact of the collision that killed her, it was the sight of the many men in uniform with pistols stuffed into the leather belts they wore beneath their bellies that took her last breath from her. As soon as the accident was reported three police cars arrived, sirens blaring and lights flashing. The officers rushed to where the truck was parked, pushed to the side of the road. A fire engine followed almost immediately, and men in helmets and yellow safety jackets climbed out, yelling instructions to the driver. Maria had hit her head on the edge of the truck's open cabin, but there was no blood, only shock and a mild ache, which could have been the sun in her eyes or the hunger in her belly. Within minutes, there was the sound of three helicopters hovering in the sky. One of them landed fairly close to the sheriff's truck. Maria was wheeled to the helicopter in the gurney that the firefighters brought with them. I don't think she lived to see the inside of the helicopter, I think she just died of the fear that froze the blood inside her and had entered her the day she chose to leave her home across the border in search of a better life.

Maria talks to me now. She says that Carlos is still in that helicopter, flying those children out to a hospital where their limbs can be stitched back again. She says that the helicopter is taking the longer route home, that it must fly over the jagged peaks of these impossible mountains before finding a flat space to land and disgorge its passengers. I know that one of the passengers is my niece, a small child with her father's laughter and her mother's soft brown eyes.

I do not want to dream anymore. I do not want to dream of a life I have lost forever. I know now that I will always be here, that I have become a part of the process of birth and death, that I have suffered and that my suffering has been acknowledged by strangers who have touched the center of my sorrow and not thought less of me for being an outsider, a stranger, Firangi Amreeki, American Stranger.

Haji Meer is obsessed with Anarguli's baby. He keeps staring at the little girl, a thin veil of longing glazing his eyes. Bulbul is annoyed and glares back at him, as if trying to beat him in the blinking game, but Haji Meer is not even aware of Bulbul's irritation. He continues to gaze at her, whispering something I cannot make out.

I am afraid that this man will grab the child and throw it into the fire. That is what I expect from a man who abandoned his own daughter. I want to tell Bulbul to protect Sahar Gul as if she was his own, but I am not sure how he will take this advice. I am not sure which way things will swing in this place, and I have learned to shroud my uncertainty in silence.

Noor Kaka sings a lullaby for the girl he has named. He was given the privilege of reciting the azaan, the call to prayers, into the baby's ears, calling her into the faith, baptizing her, so to speak. Waris placed several grains of molasses on the baby's lips to sweeten her life and her words. Sabir unwrapped his turban and offered it to Anarguli as a swaddling sheet for her daughter. Qasim took the cowrie shell that dangled from a safety pin hooked onto his shirt and set it on the baby's chest. And Bulbul placed his red scarf in Anarguli's lap, a blanket for the baby.

Anarguli smiled throughout the giving of gifts. But when she lifted Bulbul's scarf to wrap around her baby, she suddenly gave way to tears, sobbing hard, her breath catching and her shoulders shaking with unspoken grief. She crumpled into a heap and I was afraid she would suffocate her baby. Noor Jehan leaped forward and reached for the child who was screaming with distress. Bulbul looked at the baby and then at Anarguli and then at the floor. He did not move. I saw the ends of his long fingers twitching and I looked away.

It is morning now. I am getting used to this routine of taking the metal bucket outside and shoveling snow into it to melt down into water for washing and drinking. It gives me a structure to live by, and it gives me a sense of purpose in this place where nothing makes sense and nothing has a reason.

Bulbul came with me this morning to shovel the snow into the bucket. I looked at him and smiled. His mouth twitched at the corners as if wanting to return my greeting, but I could see that despite this effort, his eyes were cloaked in sorrow. We shoveled the snow in silence, each of us lost in our own thoughts.

Over these past many days (I have lost count now, and what use is time when there is nothing to measure it against?) I have come to understand what it means to live inside the landscape of one's own mind, where one can create an entire new world, keeping it secret from others. And I have also come to understand the silence of these people here, locked up in their own stories of loss and love and longing. I do not want to intrude into their thoughts, and have learned that the silence between the words they speak carries more than all the words I have ever spoken.

Bulbul began speaking after we had carried several buckets to the drums inside the room which used to be my cell. The sun's rays between noon and sunset fall obliquely into the cell, melting the snow in these drums. We carry the buckets into the kitchen only after the sun has helped us in this task of reclaiming the water. We had made our last trip to the cell when Bulbul pulled at my shirtsleeve and pointed to the charcoal drawing he had scratched onto the wall a long time ago. I could see the outline of the heart and the round face of the girl he had kissed with so much passion the day he came to talk to me, a mug of tea in his hand. I patted Bulbul on his back to acknowledge that I remembered that day, and picked up the bucket to return to the kitchen. Bulbul stopped me, pulling at the bucket and asking me to stay.

I set the bucket down and looked at Bulbul, waiting for him to tell me what he carried in the recesses of his heart. Bulbul turned away from me and began to speak.

I love that girl, brother. I love her with all my heart, and I want to embrace her with all my heart, but you saw her tears and you see the child, and you know that I have nothing to offer. How will I look after her, and how will I feed the child, clothe her, buy her books for school, find the money for her dowry? How will I honor Anarguli, how will I make her mine when she still keeps the one she loves in the folds of her heart?

She did not come here because she is crazy like Gul Agha or Haji Meer or Karim Kuchak. She came here because she had nowhere else to go, like me. And she had no one to love her, also like me, brother.

Anarguli is from a tribe which believes that the women born in it should live and die according to a strict code of honor. She was one of several daughters born of several mothers, all married to her father, an old fool who had the money to pay for a new bride every few years. Anarguli told me that her father believed it was manly to marry as many wives as one could—it signified prosperity and virility, and was good for the tribe. Of course, it would have been better for the family and the tribe if her father had sired many sons instead of a handful of daughters, one of who would wound him and bring so much disgrace to him.

Old and ailing, Anarguli's father had to hire a young man to help him with the plowing and the harvesting. Anarguli dared to fall in love with that man, the son of a poor peasant who did not own the land he tilled. She loved him as much as he loved her, and much as they knew that their marriage was an impossibility, they continued to love one another until they decided to honor that love by marrying of their own will.

Anarguli's lover asked a friend of his to perform the nikah to solemnize the marriage in the eyes of God. Once that was done he took Anarguli away, wanting to escape from her father and the disgrace that this transgression would bring upon his own family.

They fled to the city where he got a job as a roadside vendor, selling fruit and vegetables from his cart.

I saw him often when I was working for the kebab man. He was a pleasant fellow, named after our Prophet, Mohammad. He would let me pick those fruits that customers flung onto the unwanted pile. Sometimes I would take back bruised tomatoes and cucumbers to my mother who made a salad for Gulmina and me. He was a good man, and I will never forget his kindnesses to me.

I will also never forget the day he died, my brother, the day Anarguli's father found him and shot him in the crowded bazaar on a morning when my feet hurt so much I thought I should return home early because standing was so painful. But I did not go home that day, or that evening, for Mohammad had been shot, once in his head, several times in his stomach, and twice in his legs. I forgot the pain in my feet and rushed to him, brother, calling his name, shouting at Anarguli's father to let him be, to leave him alone.

But it was too late. Mohammad was dying in my arms while the crowd gathered, and I remembered my father when I found him in the field the day of his accident. I looked at Mohammad's face as he tried to speak to me. I could not understand what he was saying, so I lowered my head to his mouth. He whispered her name to me, and told me where to find her.

Anarguli's father was telling the crowd that this was the man who had dishonored him, and that killing him was the only way to reclaim his lost honor. The crowd had nothing to say—they dispersed as suddenly as they had collected, leaving me alone with the limp body of this unfortunate son of a peasant with no land and now, no honor.

I asked the kebab seller to help me bury Mohammad before sunset. Several people spat on his corpse when the story of his elopement was recounted in the bazaar, each telling more detailed and varied. The kebab man took some money from his pocket and gave it to me. He said he could use all the fruit and vegetables left on Mohammad's cart, and that I should clean the cart and carry Mohammad's body on it to the nearest cemetery.

The tandoor keeper and kebab seller lifted Mohammad's body onto his cart while I held its wheels, keeping it from sliding on the rotten peels and putrefied fruit that had collected beneath it. I flung my shawl over Mohammad's body to cover him from the prying eyes of passersby. It was that time when the sun begins to disappear beyond the mountains, and though there was a chill in the air, I did not miss the shawl.

But I missed Mohammad, and my father, and there was an ache in my heart which was more bitter than the pain that crippled my feet.

I managed to wheel the cart with Mohammad's body on it to the cemetery where I paid the keeper to quickly dig a grave before sunset. And then, after offering the fatehah prayers for the departed soul, I rushed through the busy streets to the Deh Mazang area near the university where a settlement of refugees had built shanties for their families. I ran through the lanes looking for the tea stall and the barbershop Mohammad had described to me. I found the shop and asked for the whereabouts of a certain Mahabat Khan, the man who had sheltered Mohammad and Anarguli.

At first the tea stall owner hesitated to tell me. When I began crying, saying that a young woman's life was in danger, he pointed to a small wooden door plastered over with cigarette ads. He said that I must be quick, for I may already be too late to save the life of this woman I spoke of.

I was not too late, brother. I found her on the floor of the courtyard of that small house. There was blood on the brick floor. It was already dark, but the light from the street shone into the darkness of that home. There was no one else there—I called out to her, speaking her name softly, wondering whether she could hear me, whether she was still alive.

She did not answer me. After waiting for what seemed like a lifetime, I walked toward her and kneeled down to see if she had survived the blow to her head. There was a gash on her head made by a sharp and probably heavy instrument, like an axe. There was so much blood that my shalwar was soaked at the knees where I was kneeling over her. I spoke her name several times until she opened her eyes.

I do not believe that she could see me then, brother, and it was not because of the darkness or the injury that could have taken her life. She could not see me because she did not want to see the absence of the man she had loved with all her heart.

I don't know how Anarguli came to this place, to Tarasmun. She has not spoken to me since I arrived here. But I know that in her eyes she still holds the image of her husband, the father of the child she has given birth to, Sahar Gul, the Rose of Sunrise.

ten

I am having those dreams again, and much as I try to shut out the terrible images of maimed and hopelessly injured people, I cannot. It is as if my mind's eye insists that I see these things over and over again until the limits of its endurance are stretched and I, too, lose my sanity.

Last night Haji Meer finally did what I had feared. In a sudden lunge he snatched Sahar Gul out of Anarguli's lap and clutched her close to his chest. Anarguli did not move. She only opened her mouth but no words came out. It was Gul Agha who leaped forward and tried to pry the child out of Haji's stranglehold. Haji refused to let go and kept repeating the name of his dead daughter: *Zarsanga, Zarsanga.* His eyes were wide and unblinking, and he glowered at anyone daring to come close, cursing and spitting and kicking. Waris and Sabir joined Gul Agha in his efforts to rescue the baby, and it took all their strength to pin Haji against the wall in order to recover her.

By the time they managed to loosen Haji's grip the child had stopped breathing. By some miracle of faith, or perhaps the mere application of skills I learned in that other place I no longer think of, I managed to resuscitate the baby by breathing into its tiny mouth. Anarguli flew at me and pulled at my head, clutching handfuls of hair and biting my shoulders. She was screaming, calling out her husband's name. I could taste milk on the baby's mouth and I could smell the urine that soaked its blanket. When it finally took a breath and emitted a long, drawn-out wail, there was an astonishing silence in the room. Anarguli froze again, then reached forward and grabbed the baby. She was confused and kept listening to its heartbeat. Noor Jehan assured her that Sahar Gul was alright, that she had survived her first shock of being born into madness. Anarguli smiled, it was a warm, shy sort of a smile. She looked straight at me and bowed her head and whispered her gratitude.

And then the laughter came, and the cries of relief, and the tears, and the warm acknowledgment that I was a fellow traveler, that I had suffered like them, and that I wanted to lessen their suffering in whichever way I could.

Everyone in the kitchen came and shook my hand and Karim Kuchak just wrapped himself around my legs, refusing to let go. He said he would be most faithful to me, most obedient, if only I would teach him the workings of that miracle. And Bulbul—he was the most moved of all. For a while he just stayed still in his corner, watching the little celebration of life being played out before him. After Waris and Sabir and Noor Jehan had thanked me for the hundredth time, after Noor Kaka had blessed me with a prayer and Hayat had chanted some verses over my head, Bulbul came to me and laid his head on my shoulder.

I did not know what to do when he stayed like that, almost catatonic, for a long time. It had always disgusted me, this contact between men. And I have been wary about Bulbul ever since he grabbed my hand and rolled up his trousers to show me the burn marks on his legs.

I could hear him breathing; his breath was warm against my chest. And I could feel his tears against my shirt.

When the others dispersed into their corners Bulbul shook my hand, then lowered his head and touched his eyes to the back of my hand. He did not speak. My hand was damp with his tears and I could still feel his breath on my chest.

They have strung him up in the basement with a red scarf. His eyes are holes, his mouth empty of its teeth. A dog chews something pink and wet. It is a man's tongue. Bulbul's hands have been tied and trussed up with twine, twisted behind his back. He has no feet—his legs end in stumps and his pants are rolled up to show the black marks on his skin.

His pants have been peeled away from his hips to reveal the pair of pliers which attach themselves to his testicles.

Bulbul is still breathing when I find him. He swings slowly from the rafters and hums a song, a lullaby that Noor Jehan used to sing to Qasim:

Gham de azma de ghare har day
De ghare har de zre de pasa gerzawema

The sorrow you feel is the necklace on my neck
I carry that necklace above my heart

Haji Meer came to me today, looking down at the brick floor the whole time he sat in front of me. He has been shunned by Gul Agha and the others from the basement, although Noor Jehan still gives him his daily ration of food. But ever since that incident with the baby, Haji has sort of been left on his own. No one bothers to talk to him; in fact, Karim Kuchak and Gul Agha have gone to the extent of skirting around him each time they need to pass by to get to the basement or take the food Noor Jehan dishes out from the cooking fire.

I was not comfortable when Haji sidled over and sat on his bottom in front of me. He seemed to look around himself all the time, as if he was expecting to see someone pop out from behind him and take him by surprise. But the others just stared at the walls and pretended he didn't exist.

The worst was when Haji reached for my legs and began to prostrate himself, touching his forehead against my knees and murmuring something I could not understand. The only word which was familiar was his daughter's name. He spoke her name in a voice that was choked, and I feared he would break down at any point and do something unexpected and dangerous.

I called Bulbul over, feeling quite powerless to get up and move away from him. Bulbul took awhile to come and he, too, seemed not to notice Haji Meer at my feet. I asked him to tell me what Haji was saying. Bulbul avoided looking at him but still went ahead and asked him what he wanted from me.

Tell Bacha Saheb that I would like him to bring my daughter back from her grave. Tell His Holiness that I will pay anything for him to bring my daughter back, like he brought that small rat back to life. Tell him I want him to bring Zarsanga and to breathe life into

her like he did for that small mouse that now smiles and drinks her
mother's milk and makes my life miserable because she is not mine.

Bulbul tried to explain all this to me, but somehow could not find the words to help me with the title Haji had given me: *Bacha Saheb*. I heard Haji repeating this as many times as he spoke his daughter's name, but Bulbul did not seem to think it necessary to explain their significance to me. I will ask Sabir what this means, although I should really forget about it since Haji is not quite in his senses anymore, hasn't been since making that terrible decision to let his daughter die.

I see the graves again. There are rows upon rows upon rows. Each
one is about a foot long and six inches wide. Each one has a small,
sharp stone as a marker at the head. I walk through the passages
between the graves until my feet begin to hurt. I sit myself down be-
tween two graves to catch my breath and rub my feet.

Suddenly the ground beneath me opens up and I slide slowly into
the earth. I see the graves from inside now. They are full of small, rat-
like animals, rodents of all kinds. None of these creatures are dead.
They are just waiting to dig themselves out and breathe again.

I know this in the strange way that dreams have of letting one
know things without really showing them.

The camel meat is lasting us quite a long time. I think it's because Noor Jehan boils the bones to make us soup. Some of us get the meat; others just content themselves with the broth.

I think I will be here long after the meat and the bones and the soup have disappeared.

* * *

Sabir comes to me today and tells me that he is worried that once the snow starts to melt, the attacks will begin again. He says the mountain passes will clear themselves of the ice which makes them impenetrable, within two weeks. Already he can see the great masses of ice shrink on the peaks all around us. And I know from my own work of shoveling the snow into pails that there is less and less of it.

I also know that once the snow melts we will be able to see the graves again. And we won't even know who was buried where since there were no markers to begin with, and in any case, all graves look alike when they have been dug for those who have no one to mourn them.

Last night there was a dull thud outside. I woke up and stared at the darkness for a long time. I know I had been dreaming, and I was glad to have lost the dream for it was as distressing as the rest.

I am always waiting to wake and find myself in some other place, and sometimes I am afraid that I shall never wake up and that the place of my dreams is the place where I will live, always.

Bulbul says the snow has started to melt and that a large chunk fell off the kitchen roof last night. I don't know whether this is good news or whether we should begin to fear the war again.

Much as I have tried to be at peace with my surroundings, I know that the madness of war is infinitely better than the madness of time standing still. At least in war there is a beginning and an end. Here there is

nothing, and I don't know how to live with this emptiness anymore.

Sabir says he has heard the sound of gunfire in the distance. He says he saw smoke spiraling into the sky the
other day. And he saw planes flying overhead, tiny, like
kites in the sky.

*They have come again, and this time they carry food packages and
soda cans in large blue parachute bags. I am hungry and do not wait
for them to give us the message they have brought for us. I tear into
the food package—there is peanut butter and pork rinds and soya
sauce. I find some chewing gum and a stick of licorice. And I find the
message written on the back of a baseball card:* The partnership
of nations is here to help.

*I reach for the soda and before I can open the can, it explodes in
my hand. I see my friend Gary trying to say something to me but I
cannot make out the words. My hands are just stumps now. Gary
laughs and picks up another can and throws it at me, chiding me
to make that winning layup in our game of one-on-one. He is still
laughing as I show him my stumps. The can lies at my feet, rolling on
its round belly. I lean down to look at it. There are words written on
it:* This is gonna shine like a diamond in a goat's ass.

*I look at Gary and I see his face change as something shoots out
of the air and strikes his head, severing him at the neck. Gary is still
laughing as his head falls at my feet and I lean down toward it so
that I can hear the words he is saying. He tells me that from now on
it's just a game, and that I am the only one playing it.*

I cannot deal with this anymore. Every day one of these
crazy people comes to me and asks me to heal a cut or a
bruise or an infection. Karim Kuchak follows me around

and hangs onto every word I speak. Hayat offers me her small leather pouch in which she carries dried herbs and bits and pieces of wire, hair, grass, and even what looks like animal gut. And Anarguli insists that I have to hold the baby every day in order to give it strength to survive. She has wrapped it in Bulbul's red scarf and the skin of a slaughtered lamb. Noor Jehan has brought the baby to me several times to ask me to bless it with my breath and a prayer.

I really don't understand what's going on. Bulbul tells me that they all believe I have special powers that can heal them. I am referred to as Bacha Saheb, a holy man. I ask Bulbul whether he believes all this drivel and he just nods slowly, staring at my mouth.

I don't know how long I will have to play this game now. My endurance wears thin like the ice outside, and I know I simply have to find a way to get out.

Noor Kaka has come to pay homage to me today. The old man can barely see or stand, but he can certainly see my saintliness and my special powers. He asks me to look at his eyes and tell him whether I can help his failing vision. All I see is a lot of mucus being secreted out of his tear ducts. I want to tell him that at his age, and in the middle of this war, he should just be grateful he can get around in this miserable place without stumbling over these crazies. As if reading my mind, he says he is worried he will fall and hurt his bones and then become a burden to his sons and daughter again. I want to tell him that it's time he gave it up for good, went off to his Maker who would surely let him into Heaven in exchange for the treasure he found in some godforsaken desert a hundred years ago.

* * *

Gul Agha, too, has a problem he wants to discuss. He brings me a crumpled photograph of a young boy sitting in front of a dark curtain, possibly a photo studio like the ones I saw in the city before I lost my way and my ability to reason. Gul Agha asks me to tell him if this child is still alive. And if he is, does he remember his father? Can he walk now? Has his lame leg been fixed? Maybe the good doctors at the camp made him a prosthetic limb, maybe he has a wooden leg now, maybe he will walk all this way on that wooden leg and find his father who abandoned him the day he lost his way, and lost his mind.

I am at the wall again. I have begun to assemble the rats I have freed from their graves, and like the Pied Piper, I am leading them to that part of the wall we filled in with bricks. They begin digging. I watch as they claw their way into the earth and down into its innards. There are hundreds of rats and they obey my command for I am a saint, a man with special powers.

They have dug a hole wide enough for me. I get down on my knees and crawl through to the other end. It takes awhile to get through this dark tunnel, and when I get to the other end I am facing a deep pit filled with shit.

I gag and then retch. Something falls out of my mouth with the yellow mucus. It is Noor Kaka's eyes.

The child doesn't stop crying. It screams itself to sleep every night. And during the day it whimpers and wails as if in constant pain. Bulbul says it is hungry. Noor Jehan thinks it is in pain. Hayat says it is cursed. All I want is for it to shut up and let me sleep.

* * *

Karim Kuchak asked me today if I could help him to grow and be tall like normal men. I want to laugh in his face and tell him that if I could make him grow I could also land myself a spaceship and get the hell out of here.

These people are crazier than I thought.

Waris and Sabir have asked me to help them collect as much snow as possible before it melts and is sucked into the earth. Outside I can see the smoke that Sabir spoke about. It rises from beyond the black mountains and colors the sky gray.

After we had filled up the drums with snow which is no longer white and clean, Waris came to me and asked if I could cure him of *a man's worst disease*. He does not say more than this, but from how he turns away, averting his gaze from mine, I can guess it has something to do with his crotch.

Oh boy, now I am a healer, not just a gatherer of snow and a melter of ice.

I am so tired this evening that I can hardly write, and even if I wasn't tired the crying baby doesn't let me sleep. Sometimes I wish I could just pick it up and throw it out into the courtyard.

Maybe I should never have brought it back to life.

Waris does not look at me today when we begin our task of shoveling the snow into the storage drums. I want to tell him that I could try and cure him of his disease (syphilis, impotence?) only if he got me out of here. But

he avoids me and I don't know how to bring up the sub-
ject of his diseased dick.

That's a hoot. Diseased Dick. Pickled Prick.

I can see the smoke coming from another direction now,
from a place closer to us. And today I heard the bombers flying overhead. It's only a matter of time now before
they come and get me.

I find Bulbul is really quite a funny guy. He makes me
laugh, the way he hangs around that woman and her
child, pretending he can give them a life when he doesn't
even have one of his own.

Something stinks here. Today I found several maggots
in the camel soup. Maybe Noor Jehan thinks the food
tastes better with some extra protein.

*The camel calls to me from the other side of the pit with the dead rats
floating in a river of urine. He wants me to heal the wound which
has the shape of a necklace around his long neck. I want to get closer
to him but the river is deep and wide and I am afraid I will fall in
and drown.*

Sabir says he knows the planes are coming back, carrying their lethal load of bombs. I know they carry only
peanut butter and jelly sandwiches. He says we may all
have to go back into the basement in order to be safe.

I tell him that Waris needs to have his dick fixed. I point
toward my crotch and act like I'm going to pull down my
pants so that he can have a peek. He stares at me and then
laughs. Then he stops suddenly and walks away.

Maybe tomorrow he will come to me and ask if I can grow his leg back.

The fucking child does not shut the fuck up why doesn't her stupid mother feed her or fling her into the fire so that we can sleep for God's sake.

Noor Kaka has come again with the problem of his eyes. I tell him that he should go and get himself a new pair, and the stupid man takes off his glasses and gives them to me, telling me to fix these if I can't fix his eyes.

Where the hell is your shitty treasure, old man?

oh god oh god oh god oh god they are making us move back into the basement overflowing with shit and dead rats.
I want to die, mother I want to die in a clean place and never leave home again.

I can hear the bombing. I know they have come for me, but they will first have to destroy the others since there will be place for only one on board.

I must let them know I am in the basement. They should not waste precious time looking for me, because the snow is melting and there will be a river beyond the wall which we cannot cross.

Karim Kuchak has offered to help me. He has been a good friend ever since the damned baby nearly choked to death. He follows me around like a dog and wags his tail every time I throw him a bone from my soup. He's going to help me find my radio transmitter which I know is floating at the bottom of that river outside the wall.

I like Karim Kuchak, even if he has a big head and a small body. Nobody said he was Karim Abdul-Jabbar, anyway.

I want to tell Bulbul about our plans, but I don't trust him anymore, especially after he tried to grab my crotch and fondle me the night he told me about the time he was raped outside the burger joint in that city where his uncle took him.

Brother, I was young, you know, I didn't know what the man wanted, and I got into his car because he said he would drive me to my home in the camp outside the city. I was attending to the people who came in cars to eat at the many food places in this new market built along the road to the border. I would run to fetch them a burger or a Pepsi and they would give me a tip, which I took home to my uncle. Most times, I would spend that money just trying to get home—it was a long way, and I had to take several buses and a taxi, which I would share with three other boys who worked at odd jobs like me.

But that day I thought I could save the money, and I accepted the offer of this man who had come to eat but who didn't ask me to get anything for him from the snack bar. He said he wasn't hungry for food, that he was going my way, and that he would take me home.

He did terrible things to me, brother, things that come to me in my dreams and then I don't ever want to wake up. After that night, I thought I was no longer a boy, I was useless, like a woman. I didn't tell my uncle, but he smelled the man's fluid on my shalwar and beat me till I fainted and fell on the floor.

I didn't want to wake up, brother. I wanted to stay on that floor forever, so that my shame would die along with me.

I am sick of his stories and his whining and the way he touches me. I know he is a coward and, in any case, he will never leave that love of his life and her brat baby.

Karim and I are getting out of here as soon as I can call my people to tell them where I am. Karim says he is small enough to fit into the cockpit of the smallest plane. And if there isn't any space, there's always a place in one's heart.

Whatever, Shorty.

Jesus Christ, now it's that crazy foreign woman who wants me to fix her ridiculous braid of hair onto Anarguli's head. She says she is old now, and before she dies she wants to find a place for her hair, and since Anarguli hardly has any her head should be just fine.

Jesus Jesus Jesus.

Shorty and I have a plan. We need to send him over the wall so that he can fish out my radio transmitter from the river. We can't tell Waris this because he is worried about his sick dick, and he will never let me go until I cure him. I want to tell him to put it up the dog's butt. That should fix it.

The sun is strong today and there is hardly any snow left on the ground. I can see new leaves on the tree in the middle of the courtyard. There isn't much time now. As soon as the snow melts, the bomb they left in the rubble will be set off and destroy this place. All it needs is the sun's rays to warm it up.

I need to get out of here before that. We have to find a rope to tie around Shorty who will climb that damned wall.

* * *

The children came to me again today. They were holding yellow soda cans in their hands. They said there were many more across the wall and beyond the river, near the village where a cooking fire burns all day long.

I refuse to tell Bulbul about our plans. He is not my friend anymore. He spends most of his time with that woman and her child. Good enough. There wouldn't be enough room for him in the plane anyway.

I sent Shorty on a recce mission to look for rope. I can smell the fire from across the wall as if it's burning in my heart.

In the kitchen Noor Jehan cooks that vile meat with the maggots in it. The whole place stinks of rotting flesh but no one seems to notice, and they eat that disgusting stew as if it were the best thing on earth.

Noor Kaka comes to me again and asks me if I fixed his glasses. I certainly did—I took out the broken lens and gave him the wire frame and told him he would see better now. Also that he should let me know when he finds that treasure he was telling us about.

He looked at me as if I was crazy and put the glasses back into his pocket. Let him be blind if he wants to. I fixed his glasses and now he doesn't even want them.

Shorty has found a piece of rope. It has blood crusted on it. Shorty says he found it in a corner of the compound, one end tied around a picket in the ground. I can smell the blood and I can smell the stink of the camel which these people killed and now eat as if camel meat was going out of fashion.

* * *

The children tell me that the rope is not long enough to tie around Shorty to send him over the wall. They tell me that I must ask Bulbul for his scarf so that we can tie it to the rope and then send Shorty over the wall.

I don't want to tell Bulbul about our plans. He will want to bring along that woman and her child, and there will certainly not be enough room for them on the plane. But I need his scarf, so maybe I can make a deal with him, letting him get on the plane only if he leaves the wretched woman and her cranky baby behind.

Bulbul says he will never leave the woman and her baby. He says he did that once, leaving his mother and sister, and he will never do it again. I tell him to suit himself, it's his loss. Karim Kuchak and I are out of here on the first plane to land smack bang in the middle of the damn courtyard.

Sabir told me today that several villages around us have been attacked. The smoke is from the homes that have been burned in the bombings. He knows this because the smoke tells him. And I know that 5,000-pound Bunker Busters and CBU laser-guided bombs are meant to destroy entire villages, just like Daisy Cutters are meant to clear forests, and that B52 bombers carry 1,000-pound CBU-87s as well as wind-corrected CBU-103s for soft targets and that these have a 20 percent fail rate and that the little bomblets in the Mother Bomb are her children, shining like a diamond, bringing death in a little soda can.

I know, because my friend Gary told me this before his head rolled off his neck. He was still smiling when he handed me the soda can and said: *Here's a Ramadan present for you, Johnny!*

eleven

I am not eating that camel stew anymore. When the camel asked me to join his head and neck together again, I looked at the deep cut along his throat and I saw the small, white creatures wiggling even then. I have always known that camel was full of worms; and now I'm certain those maggots are still alive and that they will burrow tunnels in my gut and live there forever.

The fat woman who cooks keeps bringing me a bowl of the vile stuff but I just turn my face away and pretend not to see her. I cannot let these people know that I have other plans, so I try not to let them see my eyes where my thoughts live and breed like ferrets.

The old man with the broken glasses (which I fixed and which he keeps in his pocket) tells me not to turn away God's bounty. So I spat in his face and told him to put his bounty where the sun don't shine.

Where on earth is his treasure? He tells me to see with the eye of the heart, and I tell him that hearts don't have eyes and eyes don't have hearts.

I tell Shorty to ask the old man this, tell him that maybe if we were to find it before we leave this place, we would be rich enough to buy a house and an SUV and a big-screen plasma TV and then all I would do is watch the football games and not have to work ever, to go to war ever, to leave home ever.

Shorty says the old man doesn't talk much and tells him only that he has great sympathy for me, a Firangi so far from home and everything that is familiar to me. I know he can't even see me without his glasses and that his eyeballs have actually fallen out of their sockets, so how can he pity me and think me crazy and pathetic? He's the blind man around here, not me.

Oh God, another one of his stories. I'm sick to death of these stories. These people here have nothing else to do except tell stories, tales made up in their endless boredom. That old man gathers the others around him and tells them about the birds and the trees and the fruit of his country, and I want to tell him to shut the hell up and stuff the birds. But he just goes on and on and I want to smash his head against the wall so that I don't hear his whiny little voice anymore.

My sons, it appears my time is near.

Yeah, about time too. And I'm not your son, thank you very much.

I must tell you about that journey my father and I took so many years ago through the valley of light, where the only sounds were the breeze passing through golden wheat fields and the cooing of pigeons in the lofts of mud houses dotting the foothills. We passed through wide avenues lined with mulberry trees and listened to the unfolding of apricot blossoms on a spring morning. We saw the clay drying on the potter's hand till even he didn't know which was his skin and which was the fine clay.

We crossed the Reg Ruwan and arrived in Begram, which overlooks the low land of Kohistan and the three rivers that cut through the land. The place we rested at was known by some as Kaffir Killa,

Fort of the Infidel, and by others as just Boorj, or Tower. This place was at an elevation, like Tarasmun, my sons, near the foot of the passes that lead to Tartary. Within a few miles of it lay the great mounds, curious remnants of former ages. These were called Tope-dura and Joolga and that is where we found the treasure, my sons.

Inside these earthen mounds were coins which were from another time. There were thousands of them, in boxes and spilling out onto the earthen floor. My father picked up a few—I wanted to fill my pockets with them so that we could eat well and possibly rest at a travelers' inn, a sarai, on the way to the summer palace, but my father did not let me. He said these were from another time, they were of no use now, and that we must not disturb the belongings of the dead, much as we would not want the living to desecrate our graves. He said that the earth is actually made up of the bones and blood of our ancestors, and that the soil is the real treasure, not the coins.

My father scooped up some of the soil and placed it in his tobacco pouch which needed to be replenished. He whispered the words, Khak e Watan, soil of the homeland, and kissed the small pouch. And then we continued on our way.

I was hungry, so my father stopped beside a river and fished for me. Fish were abundant in these waters, as much as ducks and birds inhabited the sky as if it was a home to all flying creatures. My father told me there were almost fifty kinds of birds in this area, from the large red duck to the kujeer which when stripped of its feathers has a rich, soft down left on it. My father said that if we were lucky enough to hunt a kujeer, we would have a good meal that evening and I would have a warm posteen to wear in winter.

There were so many birds there, my sons—there was the kubke e duree, a bird somewhat smaller than a turkey, belonging to the species of the red-beaked partridge. Then there was the dughdour, a kind of buzzard, hunted by the most skilled men in the land. And there were animals with fur, the gor-kun, or gravedigger, and the

202 🌼 FERYAL ALI GAUHAR

moosh-khurma, like a small fox or maybe a large cat. The most sought after was the dila khufuk, a large gray weasel with a white band around its neck. And then of course there were the lesser creatures, the huzura rat that has no tail, and the spiky-backed khar pusht, and cats with long noses, short legs, and stripes down their backs.

We could see these creatures, the wild rabbit which would make a tasty stew and give us a soft skin for a winter cap. We sensed the presence of the bear—I saw a large reddish-brown animal, like a large dog, hiding behind a tree. I don't know who was more afraid, the bear or me. And there was the red fox, and the sug e kohee, or Dog of the Hills whose young are sought after for they make good hunting companions.

There was the tibbergam, a small animal which took to the ground in winter, and a large bird called unkash which ate the flesh of dead beasts. There were sheep and goats and horses, and my father kept telling me that this was the treasure, the richness of our land, the living bounty with which we have been blessed.

I could not keep any of that treasure, my sons; it was for all of us, for future generations, the sons of my sons. But that is not the way it is now, is it, Waris Khan? Where are all these creatures now? Where is all this treasure that made our land so rich that the Firangi had to come three times to rob us, and now comes again to take away what is left?

The old man looks at me now. He can see me in the dark but I don't care. I'm wondering if those rats that live in the basement with the dead people have tails.

The old woman with the dirty teeth and foul breath has a tail and she's going to help us get out of here. She wants me to cut off her braid and attach it to the other woman's head, the one with the sniveling brat in her lap. I will do this tonight. I know the younger woman with the baby has a hole in her head—I saw it a long time ago. That is what I will tell the old woman, that her hair will live in that gash. I will not tell her that her braid is the only way out of here—that and the camel's tethering rope and the funny man's red scarf.

I have described my radio transmitter to Karim Kuchak a hundred times but he still insists on calling it a telephone. I know he's not going to find a telephone at the bottom of that river outside the wall, so I have to find a way to show him what the radio transmitter looks like. Maybe the Sears catalog that crazy guy with the funny feet gave me will have a picture of it inside.

Karim Kuchak calls me *Shah Baba Tilifoon.* It means that I am the Revered Saint of Communication Instruments. He tells me that if we never get out of here, he will build a shrine for me and place the radio transmitter at the head, where people will prostrate themselves and ask my soul to bless them.

Fat chance there is of my dying in here. And even if I do, fat chance I'm going to be blessing any of these idiots from my grave.

Why are these people looking at me like this? Why don't they just mind their own business and let me be?

I have cut out many pictures from the Sears catalog and stuck them on the wall of the kitchen so that these fools here can see what it is I'm going back to. There are kitchen blenders and women with breasts in sheer brassieres and babies in Mickey Mouse pajamas and electric lawnmowers and cool boxes for beer. I haven't found a picture of the radio transmitter yet, but there are similar-looking things that should help Karim Kuchak find it.

We have to send him over the wall very soon. I can hear the planes humming overhead, and I know they're waiting for a signal from me to either land or send down something I can climb up.

I hope it doesn't snow. And I hope that old woman with the mustache doesn't wake up when I cut off her braid with the knife she hides under it.

I haven't eaten for three days now. These people are probably keeping the good meat for themselves and trying to poison me with the maggots. But I know better than that. I'm going to be getting out of here and then they can eat the maggots themselves.

It's getting colder now. My feet are blue. The shoes the funny boy gave me have fallen apart. He asked me once to get him a pair of hiking boots from home. As if I'm going to be sending him a care package as soon as I hit the highway to Tranquility, California.

I told Karim Kuchak not to eat too much of that awful stew. I'm afraid he'll get sick and then who will go over the wall? I see him looking at me between spoonfuls, and I'm afraid that his need to eat is greater than my desperation to get out of here. He is a strange-looking creature, with wrinkled skin and the voice of a child.

Karim Kuchak is giving some of his stew to the old woman with the hair. That's good. This way she'll be too sick or too sleepy to know when I cut off her braid. And if she wakes up, the poor creature, I will just have to stick that knife into her gut and let her spill all the maggots out onto the floor. *That's what the sergeant did to that girl with the dark eyes and a body the shape of a Coke bottle after he shot her in the head and before he set her on fire so that the seed he'd planted inside her wouldn't grow and become a sniveling rat who eats human hearts and threatens to take away our way of life.*

I can't believe I've done it. It didn't take much to slice off the braid—much of it wasn't even hair. There were threads and grass and twigs and birds living in nests made of old socks and torn vests. I rolled up the braid and stuffed it under my shirt. Now all I need to do is to get that stinking piss-soaked red scarf from under that sniveling brat who sleeps next to its mother. If it wakes up and starts to bawl, it will just have to die the way it should have the day Pancake Ears tried to choke the breath out of its lungs.

The One-Legged Man tells me that the planes have bombed many villages scattered in this valley of one-legged men. He says this is the only safe place now. I look at him and see a couple of maggots crawling out of his dead eye, the one which is like a tunnel.

Maybe he's dead and the worms are consuming him like they would a corpse.

I have to find a way to get to that baby without waking it up. Maybe Funny Feet can help by keeping his huge hands on the baby's mouth while I unwrap the scarf her mother has swaddled her in.

I will make a deal with him. I will tell him that he'll get his boots and his parka and his yellow corduroys if he does this for me. I know it's easy to persuade people like him—after all, he got taken by a man just for a ride home in a taxi.

Funny Feet is in on the deal. Tonight he'll put some extra maggots in the baby's mother's stew. She'll eat these and feel drowsy and then not wake up while we take away the red scarf. Funny Feet says the baby isn't his anyway, so why should he care if it lives or keeps warm or has a mother to feed it?

It's done. I have the scarf now. It stinks, but it'll have to do. I will tie it to the camel's rope and then join both of these to the old woman's hair and then send Shorty over the wall to get the radio transmitter.

It's a good thing it's not a full moon tonight. Funny Feet and I tied Shorty to the rope and then threw him over the wall. He wasn't even afraid when we hoisted him over our heads and flung him over like a lasso. He knows I'm going to get him a job at the Barnum & Bailey circus once we get home. And there'll be lots of acts like this for him to do.

Shorty hasn't gotten back yet. Funny Feet pretends he doesn't know anything about our escape plan. He doesn't even look at me in the morning. I know we have to wait until it's dark again to wait for Shorty to tug at the rope so we can bring him in.

That river outside the wall must be deep. It's taking Shorty a long time to find the radio transmitter.

He hasn't pulled on the rope yet. I have to hide the rope

in the shadows so that the others don't see it. So I drag it around the whole damn compound, following the sun. That way the rope can hide in its own shadow and nobody will see it.

Shorty should be back tonight. I can hear the planes again. They're waiting for me to call them.

When Shorty gets back I'll ask the Washington Wizards basketball team cheerleaders to do one of their special routines for him. They came to visit us at the base and they were great, signing uniforms, sitting on bombs and having their pictures taken, girls doing their thing for the war. Hot blondes with long silky hair and long silky legs. Wouldn't Shorty just love to see their underpants when they jump up and down and cheer him?

Give me an S, Give me an H, Give me an O, Give me an R, Give me a T, Give me a Y—put it together and what do you have?

SHORTY!!!! Rah Rah Shorty! Thanks to you we're all safe in our homes!

One-Legged Man is trying to wake up Sick Dick. He's gesturing frantically toward the wall.

Shit. I hope they haven't found the rope. Where the hell is Shorty?

Sick Dick and Funny Feet are running toward the wall. Has Funny Feet told them about my plans? Has he given me away, the idiot?

They have shovels and picks in their hands and I know they're waiting for Shorty to climb down so they can kill him for helping me get away. They will kill him, they will kill him, they will kill me.

* * *

They are breaking the wall down. Oh God, they will kill Shorty when they find him with the radio transmitter and then they will come for me.

Oh God Oh God Oh God.

One-Legged Man is pushing away the chunks of mud which Sick Dick and Funny Feet have broken off the wall. They are working fast. I have to work faster to get through that gap before they get me.

Shit shit shit shit.

I tried to run. I tried hard to run as quickly as I could. I tried to run even when my feet stopped moving and my breath stopped in my gullet. They caught me at the wall, they grabbed me and held me down, pinning my arms and legs with their own, pushing my face in the dirt. There were so many of them, more than I can remember. There was Pancake Ears and Ferret Face and the boy with the orange hair and bones sticking out of his feet—and all the others who had died and we had buried. But there were others I had never seen—there were children and women and camels and sheep and mules. There were men with no arms and no legs, children with no eyes, women with no hair and no shame. They suckled babies who had no mouths, and the camels had their heads put on backward.

There were so many of them at the wall. They carried little bundles on their heads and on the backs of animals. I could see the chickens and the baby lamb, and I could smell the stink of the sweat and blood and pus that oozed out of wounds on their bodies. They asked for water and Fat Woman came forward with Deaf Boy who carried a bucket on a wooden cart with one wheel missing. Fat Woman told these people to rest in the courtyard under the tree with all its leaves sprouting and its limbs gleaming. She said there is fresh water in the well with which they can wash the blood from their wounds and the dirt from their bodies. She said that there is enough food to feed them all, that there is enough space for them to sleep, that this is a safe place; this is a place that keeps us out of harm's way, out of the way of madness.

I listened to her as she spoke to these people, helping an old woman with long hair across the pile of mud where there had been a wall. I listened to the children laughing at the camels which had already found the tree under which they would sleep. I heard the babies crying and their mothers trying to soothe them. I heard the men talk in low whispers about the burning of their homes and the planes that came every night, searching for the enemy, killing so many who never knew what the war was about.

I heard all this, and I felt my head becoming heavy with the thought that there were so many more now in this place, so many more whose graves I will have to dig, even if there is no more space for further burials.

GLORIOUS
a novel by Bernice L. McFadden
250 pages, trade paperback original, $15.95

"McFadden, in her powerful seventh novel, tells the story of Easter Bartlett as she journeys from the violent Jim Crow South to the promise of the Harlem Renaissance and the civil rights movement ... McFadden (*Sugar*) weaves rich historical detail with Easter's struggle to find peace in a racially polarized country, and she brings Harlem to astounding life ... Easter's hope for love to overthrow hate—and her intense exposure to both—cogently stands for America's potential, and McFadden's novel is a triumphant portrayal of the ongoing quest." —*Publishers Weekly*

ANNA IN-BETWEEN
a novel by Elizabeth Nunez
320 pages, trade paperback, $15.95

"A psychologically and emotionally astute family portrait, with dark themes like racism, cancer and the bittersweet longing of the immigrant." —*New York Times Book Review* (Editors' Choice)

"Nunez has created a moving and insightful character study while delving into the complexities of identity politics. Highly recommended." —*Library Journal* (*starred review*)

JESUS BOY
a novel by Preston L. Allen
368 pages, trade paperback original, $15.95

"Allen has created a consummate tragicomedy of African American family secrets and sorrows, and of faith under duress and wide open to interpretation. Perfect timing and crackling dialogue, as well as heartrending pain balanced by uproarious predicaments, make for a shout-hallelujah tale of transgression and grace, a gospel of lusty and everlasting love." —*Booklist*

"Heartfelt and occasionally hilarious, *Jesus Boy* is a tender masterpiece." —Dennis Lehane, author of *Mystic River* and *The Given Day*